Death and Fantasy

Death and Fantasy:
Essays on Philip Pullman, C. S. Lewis, George MacDonald and R. L. Stevenson

By

William Gray

CAMBRIDGE
SCHOLARS
PUBLISHING

Death and Fantasy: Essays on Philip Pullman, C. S. Lewis, George MacDonald and R. L. Stevenson, by William Gray

This book first published 2008. The present binding first published 2009.

Cambridge Scholars Publishing

12 Back Chapman Street, Newcastle upon Tyne, NE6 2XX, UK

British Library Cataloguing in Publication Data
A catalogue record for this book is available from the British Library

ISBN (10): 1-4438-1347-8, ISBN (13): 978-1-4438-1347-1

In memory of my mother

Joanna Gray, *née* MacDonald

(1925-2004)

TABLE OF CONTENTS

ACKNOWLEDGEMENTS

Chapter One first appeared in *SEL Studies in English Literature 1500-1900*, 36, 4 (Autumn 1996).

Chapter Two first appeared in *Women of Faith in Victorian Culture: reassessing 'The Angel in the House'*, Anne Hogan and Andrew Bradstock (eds) (Palgrave Macmillan, 1998).

Chapter Three first appeared in *North Wind: Journal of the George MacDonald Studies* (2004).

Chapter Four first appeared in *Journal of Stevenson Studies* 2005.

Chapter Five first appeared in *Journal of Beliefs and Values,* Vol. 18, No. 2, 1997.

Chapter Six first appeared in *English Literature, Theology and the Curriculum,* Liam Gearon (ed.) (Cassell, 1999).

Chapter Seven first appeared as a plenary presentation at the C.S. Lewis Centenary Conference at Queen's University, Belfast, 1998.

Chapter Eight first appeared in *Mythlore* 97/98 (2007).

Chapter Nine first appeared in *Time Everlasting: Representations of Past, Present and Future in Children's Literature*, Pat Pinsent (ed.) (Pied Piper Publishing, 2007).

INTRODUCTION

The present collection of essays originates in my realization, while writing *Fantasy, Myth and the Measure of Truth: Tales of Pullman, Lewis, Tolkien, MacDonald and Hoffmann*[1], that I was making regular reference to a range of journal articles and book chapters which I had produced over the previous decade. It struck me that it might be useful to have these other writings, which are all connected in one way or another with fantasy writing, conveniently available in one volume. Once I had begun to see these other shorter writings as in a sense forming one body of work, I started to notice connections between them other than their link with fantasy literature. I become conscious, with a genuinely uncanny *frisson* of surprise, that most of them were in one way or another about death. Apart from the obvious fact that two of them (Chapters Two and Five) have death in the title, and the fact that the last chapter focuses on Philip Pullman's introduction of figures called "deaths" (including "Lyra's death") into *The Amber Spyglass*, on another level most these chapters are about attempts to *deal* with death—both your own death, and that of a loved one, archetypally the death of a mother. They are also about attempts to *use* death—both your own death and that of a loved one, archetypally the death of a mother[2]—in order to achieve growth not only in a spiritual sense, but also in a psychoanalytical sense.

"Use" may not seem an appropriate verb to employ in this context, suggesting as it does some kind of instrumental view of death. However, there is no doubt that religious writers *have* presented death as a *means* to an end, and none more so than George MacDonald. Tolkien famously said of MacDonald in "On Fairy-Stories": "Death is the theme that most inspired George MacDonald"[3]. And in his account of his first encounter

---

[1] William Gray, *Fantasy, Myth and the Measure of Truth: Tales of Pullman, Lewis, Tolkien, MacDonald and Hoffmann* (Basingstoke: Palgrave Macmillan, 2008)

[2] As Freud noted in his celebrated essay "The Uncanny", two of the factors which produce the effect of uncanniness are the unconscious obsession with death and the compulsion to *repeat*. See Sigmund Freud, "The Uncanny" in *Art and Literature* (Penguin Freud Library vol. 14) (London: Penguin, 1990), p.365.

[3] J.R.R. Tolkien, "On Fairy-Stories", *Tree and Leaf; Smith of Wootton Major; The Homecoming of Beorhtnoth* (London: Unwin, 1975), p. 67; see also *The Monster*

with MacDonald's *Phantastes*, C.S. Lewis makes explicit reference to the *use* of death (for what else is baptism but the symbolic use of death for a Christian end?):

> [T]he whole book had about it... quite unmistakably, a certain quality of Death, *good* Death. What it actually did to me was to convert, even to baptise (that was where the Death came in) my imagination.[4]

While much has been written about the concept of "the good death" in the context of nineteenth century Evangelical fiction[5], MacDonald's version has perhaps more affinity with Romanticism. The Romantic principle or motif of "stirb und werde" [die and become] is perhaps most strangely expressed in MacDonald's "The Golden Key", where the flying fish voluntarily dives into the boiling pot, only to reappear as a tiny winged creature or "aëranth" (whose resemblance to a fairy U.C. Knoepflmacher seems loath to admit, preferring to liken it to a tiny angel[6]). Death as the means of new life literally looms large in *Lilith*, where much of the action takes place in a vast cemetery whose sexton is Adam, also known as Mr Raven; the action largely consists in persuading Mr Vane, the narrator and main protagonist, to lie down and die. In *Phantastes* too, death figures prominently, with the narrator and main protagonist Anodos beginning the penultimate chapter: "I was dead, and right content. I lay in my coffin, with my hands folded in peace."[7]

However the enthusiasm of Anodos for being dead strongly contrasts with Mr Vane's after all very natural reluctance to die in *Lilith*, despite knowing that it is for his own good. There is something uncomfortably close to a kind of suicidal obsession in *Phantastes*, with death being sought not so much as a means of spiritual growth, but rather as a despairing regression to an imagined state of bliss prior to the acquisition of individual personhood. This theme is discussed at some length in the

---

and the Critics and Other Essays (ed Christopher Tolkien) (London: HarperCollins, 2006), pp. 153. Hereafter cited in parentheses as *MCOE*

[4] C.S. Lewis, *George MacDonald: An Anthology* (London: Bles, 1946), p. 21.

[5] See for example Gerhard Joseph and Herbert F. Tucker, "Passing On: Death" in Herbert F. Tucker (ed.), *A Companion to Victorian Literature And Culture* (Oxford: Blackwell, 1999), p. 114, discussing Pat Jalland, *Death in the Victorian Family* (Oxford: Oxford University Press, 1996) and Philippe Aries *The Hour of Our Death* [1981] (Oxford: Oxford University Press, 1991)

[6] U.C. Knoepflmacher (ed.) *George MacDonald: The Complete Fairy Tales* (Harmondsworth: Penguin, 1999), p. 249n9.

[7] George MacDonald, *Phantastes: A Faërie Romance for Men and Women* [1858] (London: Dent Everyman, 1915), p. 230.

first essay below, "George MacDonald, Julia Kristeva and the Black Sun", which uses Kristeva's idea that the achievement of individual personhood, or a "subject position", requires in effect a kind of matricide, in order to release the self from the potentially smothering effects of the "primary maternal matrix" or "semiotic *chora*". The "black sun" which blights Anodos's wanderings in *Phantastes* is in effect Gérard de Nerval's "black sun of melancholy"[8], a mark of the depression that according to Kristeva results from the failure to negotiate a proper severance from the maternal matrix. For Kristeva, this position can result in the subject seeking a suicidal (or quasi-suicidal) loss of self by symbolically merging with a mother whose death cannot be tolerated.

The death of the mother is also central to the following chapter, "The Angel in the House of Death: Gender and Subjectivity in George MacDonald's *Lilith*", which takes up Virginia Woolf's claim in her essay "Professions for Women" that a woman's achievement of a full subject-position, especially as a writer, requires "[k]illing the Angel in the House".[9] In Woolf's own case her mother, Julia Duckworth, was the incarnation of "the Angel in the House", especially in her appearance as Mrs Ramsay in *To the Lighthouse*. The symbolic battle between the angelic Mother Eve and the unruly overreacher Lilith is re-enacted in MacDonald's late fantasy novel *Lilith*. The novel is partly about Lilith's need to learn to die, at the cost of much suffering including the amputation of her clenched fist, so that she can share the delights of post-mortem existence with Adam, Eve and the family. MacDonald's engagement in late nineteenth century debates relating to gender roles is clearly apparent in *Lilith*.

Lilith was published in 1895, a year after the death of Robert Louis Stevenson. The great length of MacDonald's writing career (particularly in contrast to Stevenson's relatively short one) is illustrated by the fact that *Phantastes* was published in the year Stevenson celebrated his eighth birthday. MacDonald was already a "name" to the young Stevenson, and the little-known influence of MacDonald on the younger writer is explored in Chapter Three, "Strange Case of Dr MacDonald and Mr Hyde: RLS and George MacDonald". A central claim in this chapter is that there is a hitherto unremarked influence of MacDonald's *Phantastes* on a crucial sequence near the beginning of *Strange Case of Dr Jekyll and Mr Hyde*,

---

[8] See Nerval's "El Desdichado", cited by T.S. Eliot in *The Waste Land*, line 430.

[9] See Virginia Woolf, "Professions for Women" in Stephen Greenblatt and M.H. Abrams (eds), *The Norton Anthology of English Literature* vol. 2 (Eighth Edition) (New York: W.W. Norton, 2006), p. 2153.

when we first encounter Mr Hyde in Enfield's account of how Hyde callously trampled a little girl underfoot. Another rather neglected (if not exactly unremarked) aspect of Stevenson's *oeuvre* is his predilection for the *Märchen* or fairy tale. Stevenson's plans to publish a collection of *Märchen* were undermined by a kind of collusion (if not conspiracy) between his literary agent (Sidney Colvin), his publisher (Cassell) and his wife Fanny. Chapter Four, "The Incomplete Fairy Tales of Robert Louis Stevenson", shows how Stevenson's projected book of *Märchen* was derailed, and how instead of the book Stevenson wanted, a few fairy-tale-like (or *märchenhaft*) pieces appeared in a context that Stevenson had explicitly rejected. This chapter also discusses how Stevenson's approach in several of these *märchenhaft* tales relates to the genre of fantasy, as defined by Tzvetan Todorov, Rosemary Jackson, and Maria Nikolajeva.

Neither C.S. Lewis nor Tolkien had much time for Stevenson— Tolkien said in "On Fairy-Stories" that *Treasure Island* "left me cool" (*MCOE* 134). It would perhaps have surprised them to read Stevenson's homage to William Morris both in his story "The Waif Woman" and also in an unpublished letter to Morris[10], both discussed in Chapter Four below. Both Tolkien and Lewis were heavily influenced by Morris, and especially by his love of Northern myth. As an alternative to *Treasure Island* (and indeed the *Alice* books), the young Tolkien found that "the land of Merlin and Arthur was better than these, and best of all the nameless North of Sigurd and the Völsungs, and the prince of dragons." (*MCOE* 134-5) Tolkien continues:

> The dragon had the trade-mark *Of Faërie* written plain upon him. In whatever world he had his being it was an Other-world. Fantasy, the making or glimpsing of Other-worlds, was the heart of the desire of Faërie. (*MCOE* 135)

It was only gradually that Tolkien and Lewis realized that they shared this secret addiction to Norse mythology and fantasy writing. This realization of their common addiction to Faërie and Nordic mythology was an important factor in the founding of "The Inklings". I have devoted a substantial chapter to Tolkien in my *Fantasy, Myth and the Measure of Truth*, but he figures in a more peripheral way in the present book. Lewis by contrast dominates the present book, appearing in the last five chapters either as the main subject, or alongside MacDonald and Pullman.

---

[10] Bradford A. Booth and Ernest Mehew (eds), *The Letters of Robert Louis Stevenson* (in 8 volumes) (New Haven: Yale University Press, 1994-5), vol. 7, p. 236. See also vol. 3, p. 253.

Lewis's strategies for dealing with the impact of his mother's death form the heart of Chapter Five, "Death, Myth and Reality in C.S. Lewis". This paper, first given at a Religious Studies conference on the theme of "Death", discusses not only the ways in which the heartbroken boy from Belfast haunts the pages of *The Chronicles of Narnia*, but also the ways in which that original traumatic bereavement was uncannily repeated in Lewis's loss, again to cancer, of his wife Joy, also a mother of two sons. *A Grief Observed* was written, Lewis says, as "a defence against total collapse".[11] The graphic realism of Lewis's writing in this thinly-disguised confessional work is striking; however Lewis still seems ready to invoke myth and fantasy literature (if one can thus designate Dante's *Commedia*), not so much as a form of escape but rather as a way of somehow attempting to deal with his grief. The readiness to recognize that fantasy (or perhaps more technically "phantasy") can be a strategy for coming to terms with reality thorough a process of mourning, rather than merely being a form of delusional escapism, could be said to characterize the psychoanalytical work of the so-called "British" school of psychoanalysis, especially the work of Melanie Klein and D.W. Winnicott. I introduce some psychoanalytical ideas into this chapter, including brief references to Julia Kristeva, who, as I argue in the first chapter of the book, can play an important role in linking the insights of the British school of psychoanalysis with those of the so-called "French Freud", at least in a general sense, if not in the more peculiar senses the Lacanian "école freudienne".

Kristeva, together with Klein and Winnicott, also figures in Chapter Seven, "The Lion, The Witch and the Atlantean Box: Psychoanalysis and Narnia Revisited". This paper was given at the C.S. Lewis Centenary Conference at Queen's University, Belfast, in the same year (1998) that my book on Lewis appeared.[12] Both book and conference paper explore the intriguing (and psychoanalytically suggestive) provenance of Uncle Andrew's magic rings, made out of dust (intimations of Pullman's "Dust"?) contained in a box from Atlantis, and inherited from Mrs Lefay, Uncle Andrew's fairy godmother. The reluctance of Digory's mother to talk about this witch-like relative[13] foreshadows the reticence of Petunia Dursley on the subject of her own wizarding family connections. One of the older Lewis scholars present at the Belfast Centenary conference

---

[11] C.S. Lewis, *A Grief Observed* [published under the pseudonym N.W. Clerk 1961; reprinted under Lewis's name in 1964] (London: Faber, 1966), p.47.

[12] William Gray, *C.S. Lewis* (Plymouth: Northcote House, 1998).

[13] C.S. Lewis, *The Magician's Nephew* (Harmondsworth: Puffin, 1963), p.22.

(sadly I can no longer recall which) mentioned over dinner a phrase—"the pothological argument"—which he said he had invented as a name for Lewis's version of the ontological argument. According to Lewis, if you follow desire (symbolized by the Greek god "Pothos") wherever it leads, you will ultimately find God. Lewis himself explained what he called "the dialectic of Desire" in his Preface to *The Pilgrim's Regress*: "The dialectic of Desire, faithfully followed, would retrieve all mistakes, head you off from all false paths, and force you not to propound, but to live through, a sort of ontological proof."[14] This theme, which is pursued in Lewis's first published prose work, *The Pilgrim's Regress*, reappears in one of the last things he wrote, the posthumously published *Letters to Malcolm: Chiefly on Prayer*, when he describes the "secret doctrine that *pleasures* are shafts of the glory as it strikes our sensibility".[15] A proper response to such pleasures or "tiny theophanies" is, according to Lewis, to say: "What must be the quality of that Being whose far-off and momentary coruscations are like this!" For, he continues, "[o]ne's mind runs back up the sunbeam to the sun."[16] This passage is cited in Chapter Six below, "Spirituality and the Pleasure of the Text: C.S. Lewis and the Act of Reading", which explores how this "secret doctrine" of pleasure can be related to the experience of reading, and contrasted with the pretensions of "spirituality" satirized by Lewis in *The Screwtape Letters* and *Perelandra*.

I have argued elsewhere that, in his strong criticisms of C.S. Lewis, Philip Pullman may underestimate the *dialectical* nature of Lewis's Platonism.[17] It is the controversial relationship between Lewis and Pullman that dominates the final two chapters below. That relationship is explored in Chapter Eight, "Pullman, Lewis, MacDonald and the anxiety of influence", a version of which was originally given at the George MacDonald Centenary conference at the University of Worcester in 2005. This essay seeks to show how a series of strategic (if, according to Bloom, unconscious) *misreadings* constitutes Pullman's literary filiation from Lewis, and Lewis's from George MacDonald. That trio of fantasy writers also forms the basis of Chapter Nine, "Witches' Time in Philip Pullman, C.S. Lewis and George MacDonald". This chapter is a version of a paper

---

[14] Preface to the Third Edition of *The Pilgrim's Regress*, in C.S. Lewis, *Selected Books* (London: HarperCollins, 2002), p.9.
[15] C.S. Lewis, *Letters to Malcolm: Chiefly on Prayer* [1964] (London: Collins Fount, 1977), p.90. See also *Selected Books*, p. 280.
[16] *Letters to Malcolm*, pp. 91-2. See also *Selected Books*, p. 281.
[17] William Gray, *Fantasy, Myth and the Measure of Truth: Tales of Pullman, Lewis, Tolkien, MacDonald and Hoffmann*; and "Pullman, Lewis, MacDonald and the anxiety of influence", Chapter Eight below.

given at the 2006 IBBY/NCRCL conference at Roehampton University on the theme of "Time Everlasting: Representations of Past, Present and Future in Children's Literature". It starts with an exploration of the ways Pullman uses the extreme longevity of the witches in Lyra's world to introduce younger readers to questions of time, and thus inevitably of death. These are essentially philosophical issues, and I argue that one of the great contributions of these (and other) writers of children's fantasy literature is to trust in the capacity of younger readers to engage with big philosophical questions (something professional philosophers seem increasingly reluctant to do). Lewis records being reminded by Owen Barfield that philosophy wasn't merely a *"subject"* for Plato.[18] Unsurprisingly, this chapter ends with reference to Plato, to whose ideas the works of MacDonald, Lewis and Pullman are, I suggest, ultimately a series of footnotes, even if Pullman's footnotes are distinctly critical—to which I would respond, and so the Platonic dialogue continues …

In reprinting these essays I have resisted the temptation to rewrite them. The odd tweak was irresistible, but for the most part I have let them stand, warts and all.[19] At some points there are inevitable overlaps, as when I return to a key theme or passage (for example the "temptation scene" in *The Magician's Nephew*) in a different context and perhaps from a slightly different angle.[20] I may also seem to offer divergent interpretations, for example, in discussing the conclusion of Lewis's *The Last Battle*. While it may well be that I have changed my mind about a particular issue, any inconsistency may perhaps be excused as a merely venial sin on the grounds of mitigating circumstances. The highly charged rhetoric which permeates the debates surrounding Philip Pullman's vilification of Lewis makes it hard to resist being drawn into the Bloomian Oedipal struggle between Lewis and Pullman: if Pullman misreads Lewis (just as, I argue in Chapter Eight, Lewis misread MacDonald), the unconscious temptation to misread Pullman and reread Lewis is powerful. Thus in Chapter Five, "Death, Myth and Reality in C.S. Lewis", which is based on a paper given in 1997 before I was acquainted with Pullman's work, I criticized Lewis's

---

[18] C.S. Lewis, *Surprised by Joy: The shape of my early life* [1955] (London: Collins Fontana, 1959), p. 180.

[19] In her article "'I am spinning this for you, my child': Voice and Identity Formation in George MacDonald's Princess Books", *The Lion and the Unicorn*, September 2004 (Vol. 28, No. 3), Ruth Y. Jenkins offered constructive criticism of my article "George MacDonald, Julia Kristeva and the Black Sun".

[20] There is also overlapping or repetition in references, due to the fact that, since this is a collection of essays, it cannot be assumed that the essays will be read in the sequence in which they are published here.

apparent trivialization of the children's deaths in *The Last Battle*. But in my 2006 paper "Witches' Time in Philip Pullman, C.S. Lewis and George MacDonald", I found myself almost defending Lewis against Pullman's charge that: "For the sake of taking them off to a perpetual school holiday or something, he kills them all in a train crash. I think that's ghastly. It's a horrible message."[21] I don't think there is necessarily a contradiction between on the one hand querying Lewis's trivializing description of a fatal rail crash including the miraculous disappearance of a sore knee caused by "a hack at rugger", and on the other hand querying Pullman's accusation that the whole ending of *The Last Battle* (indeed of the entire *Chronicles of Narnia*) is "ghastly" and "horrible". Nor do I believe that it is mere equivocation to point out that the first accusation (mine) is directed towards a kind of patronizing authorial cackhandedness on Lewis's part, with the loss of an appropriate tone and register, while the second accusation (Pullman's) is one of moral outrage at Lewis's metaphysics. Disagreeing in some respects with Pullman's reading of Lewis's metaphysics is presumably not incompatible with finding fault with Lewis's narrative competence in his writing for children.

---

[21] Susan Roberts's interview with Philip Pullman for Christian Aid, November 2002 [http://www.surefish.co.uk/culture/features/pullman_interview.htm] quoted in Hugh Rayment-Pickard, *The Devil's Account: Philip Pullman and Christianity* (London: Darton Longman and Todd, 2004), p.45.

CHAPTER ONE

GEORGE MACDONALD, JULIA KRISTEVA AND THE BLACK SUN

Most of the main critical readings of George MacDonald's *Phantastes* have recognized that the text is highly susceptible of a Freudian or (more frequently) a Jungian interpretation. Robert Lee Wolff's ground-breaking book *The Golden Key: A Study of the Fiction of George MacDonald* is, if perhaps not actually a "vulgar" Freudian reading, then certainly an example of what Norman Holland has called "first phase" psychoanalytic criticism, intent on disinterring the latent content (the game of "hunt the phallic symbol" popular in first year seminars in university "theory" courses).[1] But however unsatisfactory Wolff's psychoanalytic reading of *Phantastes* may have been, it does not seem necessary on that account to turn instead (as Edmund Cusick has argued) to Jungian psychology.[2] Unlike some other commentators (for example Richard Reis, Colin Manlove and William Raeper) who seem to take it for granted that Carl Jung's approach and terminology have some kind of natural resonance with MacDonald's writing,[3] Cusick does actually *argue* that we need to choose between the Freudian and Jungian approaches, and that the latter is more helpful. Cusick concedes that his opposition between Sigmund Freud

---

[1] Robert Lee Wolff, *The Golden Key: A Study of the Fiction of George MacDonald* (New Haven: Yale University Press 1961); Norman N. Holland, "Literary Interpretation and Three Phases of Psychoanalysis," *CritI* 3, 2 (Winter 1976) and reprinted in Alan Roland (ed.), *Psychoanalysis, Creativity and Literature*, (New York: Columbia University Press, 1978), pp. 233–47.

[2] Edmund Cusick, "George MacDonald and Jung" in William Raeper (ed.), *The Gold Thread: Essays on George MacDonald,* (Edinburgh: Edinburgh University Press, 1990), pp. 56–86, 57–9.

[3] Richard Reis, *George MacDonald* (New York: Twayne Books, 1972); C. N. Manlove, *Modern Fantasy: Five Studies* (Cambridge: Cambridge University Press, 1975); William Raeper, *George MacDonald* (Tring: Lion, 1987). A decade after the first appearance of this piece, I'd be less inclined to disagree with them. Doubtless a Jungian would have told me so.

and Jung is very crude, but somehow he seems to want to blame this on Wolff.[4] However, the fact that in 1961 Wolff was interested in the latent content of MacDonald's work hardly seems to justify Cusick in suggesting thirty years later that Freudian approaches *as such* are "biological, deterministic and negative"[5] and seemingly only interested in latent content, thus leaving the Jungian approach as the only viable option.

On the contrary, there have of course been major developments in Freudian approaches since the first phase id-psychology and its rather narrow concern with latent content. The term "Freudian approaches" should surely include the work not only of Anna Freud, Melanie Klein, Donald Winnicott, and Erik Erikson, but also of Jacques Lacan and Julia Kristeva (not to mention the later writings of Freud himself). Indeed *pace* Cusick and the Jungians, it seems to me that the best reading of MacDonald in terms of depth psychology is still that sketched out by David Holbrook in his 1983 introduction to *Phantastes,* a reading which is certainly Freudian, though it is heavily influenced by the British "object relations" school, and especially by Winnicott.[6] Holbrook's interpretation focuses on the themes of death, melancholy, and the longing for a lost maternal love, and in particular reads *Phantastes* as a quest for what was lost in a premature and traumatic weaning. Even apart from the remarkable biographical evidence we happen to have to support such a reading,[7] it is difficult to resist Holbrook's interpretation of the novel as a quest for the beginnings of being or identity in what Erik Erikson called "the primary maternal matrix"—or we might call, following Kristeva, the "semiotic *chora*", a term for the original "womb' or "receptacle" that Kristeva derives from Plato's *Timaeus.*[8] Rather than rehearse Holbrook's argument here, I propose to take further his psychoanalytical reading of *Phantastes*

---

[4] Cusick, "George MacDonald and Jung", p. 58.

[5] Ibid.

[6] David Holbrook, Introduction to *Phantastes*, by George MacDonald (London: Everyman Paperback, 1983) pp. vi–xxv. Holbrook subsequently published *A Study of George Macdonald and the Image of Woman* (New York: Edwin Mellen, 2000).

[7] In a secret drawer in MacDonald's desk were found, after his death, a lock of his mother's hair and a letter by her containing the following reference to his premature weaning: "I cannot help in my heart being very much grieved for him yet, for he has not forgot it . . . he cryed desperate for a while in the first night, but he has cryed very little since and I hope the worst is over now." See Greville MacDonald, *George MacDonald and His Wife* (London: George Allen and Unwin, 1924), p. 32.

[8] On the "semiotic" and the "*chora*" see Julia Kristeva, *Revolution in Poetic Language* (trans. Margaret Waller) (New York: Columbia University Press, 1984); extracts in *The Kristeva Reader* (ed Toril Moi) (Oxford: Blackwell, 1986).

by using some themes from the writings of Kristeva. Although Kristeva is influenced by Lacan, she also departs from him in certain respects, and links back in some interesting ways precisely to those "object relations" theorists (Klein, W.R.D. Fairbairn and Winnicott) who influenced Holbrook. The texts by Kristeva which seem to link most interestingly with *Phantastes* are: *Powers of Horror: An Essay on Abjection*; *Tales of Love*; and, above all, *Black Sun: Depression and Melancholia*.

The opening of *Phantastes* could be described in several respects as liminal, that is, having to do with the borderline. The hero, whose name Anodos means "pathless" or also perhaps "the way up" or "the way back," has just reached the age of twenty-one, and has been invested with various legal rights, including access to his late father's papers contained in an old desk or "secretary". However, this so-to-speak transition into the "symbolic order" is far from straightforward; there is something uncanny in these opening pages, a sense of anxiety. Anodos is driven by a curiosity about his father's personal history to break into a secret compartment in the secretary where he finds some withered rose leaves, a small packet of papers, and a "tiny woman-form" who proceeds to berate men, who are, she says, only convinced by "mere repetition". "But I am not going to argue with you" she says "but to grant you a wish."[9] The wish, however, is never put into words, but is rather conveyed by a sigh—the sigh with which Anodos had on the previous evening answered his sister's question about Fairyland, after she had read him a fairy-tale. Fairyland, in MacDonald's writing, has to do with the pre-linguistic, or with Kristeva's "semiotic"[10], and is very much the realm of "the mothers". As Anodos's fairy grandmother points out, while he may know something about his male ancestors, he knows very little about his great-grandmothers on either side. When Anodos again tries to argue with her, she replies: "Never mind what I seem to think. You shall find the way into Fairy Land tomorrow. Now look into my eyes." (*Ph* 5) Eagerly Anodos does so: "They filled me with an unknown longing. I remembered somehow that my mother died when I was a baby. I looked deeper and deeper, till they spread around me like seas, and I sank in their waters. I forgot all the rest." (*Ph* 5) Anodos has a vision of a sea "sweeping into bays and round capes and islands, away, away, I know not whither" (*Ph* 5). But this suggestion of *jouissance,* of an ecstatic loss of self in the unlimited, in the "oceanic feeling," is a mirage: "Alas! it was no sea, but a low bog burnished by the moon." (*Ph*

---

[9] George MacDonald, *Phantastes: A Faërie Romance for Men and Women* [1858] (London: Dent Everyman, 1915), p. 4. Subsequent references are to this edition and will be cited as *Ph* parenthetically in the text

[10] See footnote 8 above.

6)[11] The "imaginary" is a kind of fiction, and the "real" not so easily encountered.

Anodos's journey begins when his room quite literally dissolves into Fairyland. The figures in his carpet, which he had himself designed in imitation of grass and daisies, "bent and swayed with every motion of the changeful current, as if they were about to dissolve with it, and forsaking their fixed form, become fluent as the waters" (*Ph* 7). The realm of representation, of which Anodos had thought himself in control, what we might call with Kristeva (following Lacan) the realm of the "symbolic", begins to slip and slide into what Kristeva says in *Tales of Love* is "the very space of metaphorical shifting".[12] Here we move into a realm that is, as we shall see, not able to be represented, but only evoked in sound, rhythm, colour, music, above all poetry; the realm of the semiotic, "the maternal vessel," where "metaphor ... as if to blur all reference ... ends up as synesthesia".[13]

Anodos's first encounter in Fairyland is with a rather strange country maiden who informs him of what to expect from the various trees that turn out to be some of the major characters in *Phantastes*. The main villains are the Ash who is an ogre and the Alder who "will smother you with her web of hair, if you let her near you at night" (*Ph* 10). In this and the following chapter, the threatening presence of the Ash gradually intensifies, culminating in a genuinely chilling account of a chase through the woods when the Ash almost catches up with Anodos. Characteristic of the Ash are his admittedly rather phallic fingers—described as "bulbous," with "knotty joints and protuberances"—which contribute to Holbrook's interpretation of the Ash in oedipal terms.[14] However such a reading does not altogether fit what is most striking and uncanny in the appearance of the Ash; he has no centre: "I saw the strangest figure; vague, shadowy, almost transparent, in the central parts, and gradually deepening in substance towards the outside, until it ended in extremities capable of casting such a shadow as fell from the hand, through the awful fingers of which I now saw the moon." (*Ph* 30–1) MacDonald was fond of playing around with the categories of outside/inside; here he seems to be saying that the Ash has no inside or, as it is put later, "has a hole in his heart that nobody knows of but one or two; and he is always trying to fill it up, but he cannot. That must be what he wanted you for." (*Ph* 35) Rather than

---

[11] Some editions of *Phantastes* read "a low *fog* burnished by the moon".

[12] Julia Kristeva, *Tales of Love,* (trans. Leon S. Roudiez) (New York: Columbia University Press, 1987), p. 38.

[13] Julia Kristeva, *Tales of Love*, pp. 277–8.

[14] David Holbrook, Introduction to *Phantastes*, p. xix.

identifying the Ash as an avenging oedipal father-figure, one might take literally the indication that he is not yet a man, or in psychoanalytical terms, not yet an "object". The Ash seems more like Kristeva's "abject", that which is not yet clearly one thing or another, that which has not yet separated out into an object or a subject, and whose threat resides precisely in this borderline, undecided status in which the inside is not clearly demarcated from the outside. The abject can also pose in a primitive way threats that only crystallize more sharply at the oedipal stage. Thus the threatening Ash may *anticipate* the avenging oedipal father-figure, but the anxiety and terror here is perhaps more to do with the mother, or more precisely with the mother-infant dyad (since the mother at this stage has not yet become a separate object). Since the inside is still all mixed up with the outside (or the processes of projection and introjection are in continual flux), the terrifying greed and aggression are as much *in the infant* at the breast as in the mother. As MacDonald writes: "[the eyes] seemed lighted up with an infinite greed. A gnawing voracity which devoured the devourer, seemed to be the indwelling and propelling power of the whole ghostly apparition. I lay for a few moments simply imbruted with terror." (*Ph* 31–2) This is surely in psychoanalytical terms a classic case of the "biter bit".

Anodos is saved from the Ash by the entrance of the Beech. Again this has been read as the appearance of the oedipal mother; even the fact that the beech-woman is "rather above the human size" is interpreted as indicating the perspective of a child towards his mother (*Ph* 33).[15] But again we might take literally the statement that the Beech is not yet a woman (*Ph* 34). The Beech seems to embody the holding, the giving, the lulling, the sweetly sensual aspects of the "maternal vessel", the *chora*. What pervades this section is her "low, musical, murmuring voice," which is "like a solution of all musical sounds," and blends in with the sound of the wind in the leaves (*Ph* 34). Then the Beech sings "a strange, sweet song" which, Anodos says, "I could not understand, but which left in me a feeling like this—": a short poem follows, after which Anodos says he cannot put any more of it into words (*Ph* 36). This is a move typical of MacDonald in which (partly perhaps out of an insecurity about his own poetic talent) he claims to offer an inferior version of an original which in its quality, and indeed in its sometimes unknown language, is very different from what the reader is actually given. His own poetry is presented as a pale imitation of some transcendent "song without words". This idea is related to another favorite MacDonald device of running

---

[15] David Holbrook, Introduction to *Phantastes*, p. xvii.

natural sounds and rhythms in and out of language. The music of the beech-tree reappears in the final page of the novel: "I began to listen to the sounds of the leaves overhead. At first, they made sweet inarticulate music above; but, by-and-by, the sound seemed to begin to take shape, and to be gradually moulding itself into words, till at last, I seemed able to distinguish these, half-dissolved in a little ocean of circumfluent tones." (*Ph* 237) Here again we seem on the borders of the semiotic. MacDonald's actual poetry may be unremarkable; what is remarkable is the extent to which he privileges the poetic, in a gesture that certainly harks back to Novalis, and also seems to hint forward to Kristeva.

After some further wandering through the woods in which, in the best German Romantic tradition, Anodos "began to feel in some degree what the birds meant in their songs, though [he] could not express it in words, anymore than you can some landscapes" (*Ph* 39), he stumbles into a small cave, in a manner reminiscent of the opening dream sequence of *Heinrich von Ofterdingen*. As in the latter, the cave contains a well or basin with obviously magical properties; and like Heinrich's cave, Anodos's "antenatal tomb" (*Ph* 44) contains an image of his ideal woman "more near the face that had been born with me in my soul, than anything I had seen before in nature or art" (*Ph* 43). But Anodos's image of the ideal woman takes the form not of nature (as in Heinrich's "blue flower") but of art; it is a reclining marble statue, locked in a block of alabaster. After failing to penetrate his ideal woman with his knife, Anodos resorts to the magical power of song to release her. Again this sequence has been read in fairly vulgar Freudian terms, and sometimes it is obviously true that a knife is not just a knife. But it is again interesting to take a step back from the oedipal scenario where the marble woman is the inaccessible, frigid love object, to the pre-oedipal dyad where the frozen woman represents not only the withheld maternal body (or breast) but also the frozen "false self" of the baby. It is only the power of the semiotic that can break open the castrating hold of the oedipal/symbolic, as well as counteracting the more primitive denial of the maternal body/breast that is also the denial of the emerging infantile self. It is not a case of playing off the pre-oedipal against the oedipal; the former is the condition of the possibility of the latter. And the revolution of poetic language needs to be perpetual, for as soon as the frozen maternal body has been released by the semiotic pulse of song, it is immediately lost again, leaving Anodos in despair by the forsaken cave.

Anodos sets off in quest of his "white lady," and almost immediately comes across the Knight, Sir Percival, about whom he had previously read in the fairy cottage, and who in his rusty armour is literally a picture of dejection or perhaps of abjection. In his defiled armor, Percival is an outsider, "jettisoned from the symbolic system" as Kristeva puts it in *Powers of Horror*,[16] and also uncannily like the disinherited Knight of Gérard de Nerval's "El Desdichado" ("The Disinherited") which gives Kristeva her title *Black Sun*.[17] Percival's problem is that he has been tainted by his encounter with the evil Alder-maiden. Anodos has been warned. As he continues his quest for his lost lady of the marble, he experiences an ecstatic sense of union with Mother Earth: "Earth drew me towards her bosom: I felt as if I could fall down and kiss her." (*Ph* 50) "In the midst of this ecstasy" the idea that somewhere his lady was "waiting (might it not be?) to meet and thank her deliverer in a twilight which would veil her confusion" turns the whole night into "one dream-realm of joy" (*Ph* 51). The very thought of such a night of love leads to an involuntary semiotic outburst of song, which draws the response near to him of "a low delicious laugh … not the laugh of one who would not be heard, but the laugh of one who has just received something long and patiently desired—a laugh that ends in a low musical moan" (*Ph* 52). Announcing herself as indeed his "white lady", and thus "sending a thrill of speechless delight through a heart which all the love-dreams of the preceding day and evening had been tempering for this culminating hour" (*Ph* 52), the mysterious female figure invites Anodos to her grotto. There she entrances him with a tale of love: "I listened till she and I were blended with the tale; till she and I were the whole history… What followed I cannot clearly remember. The succeeding horror almost obliterated it." (*Ph* 55)

---

[16] Julia Kristeva, *Powers of Horror: An Essay on Abjection*, (trans. Leon S. Roudiez) (New York: Columbia University Press, 1982), p. 65.
[17] Julia Kristeva, *Black Sun: Depression and Melancholia*, (trans. Leon S. Roudiez) (New York: Columbia University Press, 1989). Subsequent references to this edition will be cited parenthetically as *BS*. The first quatrain of "El Desdichado" runs as follows:

> Je suis le ténébreux, le veuf, l'inconsolé
> Le prince d'Aquitaine à la tour abolie;
> Ma seule étoile est morte, et mon luth constellé
> Porte le soleil noir de la mélancolie

> I am saturnine, bereft, disconsolate,
> The Prince of Aquitaine whose tower has crumbled;
> My lone star is dead, and my bespangled lute
> Bears the black sun of melancholia.
> (translation as in the English version of *Black Sun* by Leon S. Roudiez, p. 140).

This horror is the replacement of the damsel by "a strange horrible object" that looks like "an open coffin set on one end" (*Ph* 55). This hollow, rough representation of the human frame seems made of decaying bark, which is seamed "as if [it] had healed again from the cut of a knife" (*Ph* 55). This "thing" literally displays the back-side of the enchantress. The obvious Freudian reading of this is that it expresses a horror and disgust of the vagina both as a displaced anus and as the site of castration. However, it is also possible to read this passage in the light of Kristeva's work on depression and melancholia, especially as this scene with the Alder-maiden marks the outset of Anodos's depression. Kristeva writes in *Black Sun*: "The depressed narcissist mourns not an Object but the Thing. Let me posit the 'Thing' as the real that does not lend itself to signification, the centre of attraction and repulsion, seat of the sexuality from which the object of desire will become separated." (*BS* 13) Kristeva continues in a way that uncannily echoes the movement of MacDonald's narrative: "Of this Nerval provides a dazzling metaphor that suggests an insistence without presence, a light without representation: the Thing is an imagined sun, bright and black at the same time." (*BS* 13) Indeed, what she writes next could almost be summary of the plot of *Phantastes*:

> Ever since that archaic attachment the depressed person has the impression of having been deprived of an unnameable, supreme good, of something unrepresentable, that perhaps only devouring might represent, or an *invocation* might point out, but no word could signify … Knowingly disinherited of the Thing, the depressed person wanders in pursuit of continuously disappointing adventures and loves; or else retreats, disconsolate and aphasic, alone with the unnamed Thing. The "primary identification" with the "father in individual prehistory" would be the means, the link that might enable one to become reconciled with the loss of the Thing. Primary identification initiates a compensation for the Thing and at the same time secures the subject to another dimension, that of imaginary adherence, reminding one of the bond of faith, which is just what disintegrates in the depressed person. (*BS* 13–4)

We will have cause to refer back to this passage in our reading of MacDonald's text. But already here it is significant that the figure who saves Anodos from the "unfathomable horror" of the Alder-maiden, and the Ash "with his Gorgon-head" who now appears, turns out to be the Knight, figuring as "the father in individual prehistory" who precedes and makes possible the subsequent oedipal father of the symbolic order (*BS* 56).

However, although saved from "unfathomable horror" by the as yet unnamed Knight, Anodos enters the depression that will haunt the remainder of the book. The daylight has become hateful to him, "and the thought of the great, innocent, bold sunrise unendurable" (*Ph* 57). The birds are singing, but not for him. After an interlude in a farm-house which contains one of the many nurturing mothers in the book, Anodos comes to a different kind of house containing a different kind of mother: this is the house of the ogre, or as it will later be called, "the Church of Darkness." The epigraph to this chapter is from the "Mother Night" speech of Mephistopheles in Goethe's *Faust:* "I am a part of the part, which at first was the whole."[18] The epigraph is directly relevant to this chapter, for Anodos finds in this house a woman reading aloud from "an ancient little volume" what amounts to a kind of hymn to darkness. This could certainly be seen as an inversion of Christian Orthodoxy, and seems in part to be derived from the passage from *Faust* that provides this chapter's epigraph. But there is another, perhaps less obvious, intertext at this point. For what the woman reads in the ancient volume bears a strong resemblance to Novalis's *Hymns to the Night*, which MacDonald must have known in the 1850s and would later translate (in 1852 he had already published a translation of Novalis's *Spiritual Songs*). We may go with the Goethe intertext, in which Mephistopheles, the "spirit of negation" ("*der Geist der stets verneint*"), is the unwilling servant of the greater good, and darkness ultimately assists in the triumph of light; or we may go with the Novalis intertext in which night is positively hymned as the great Mother. In neither case is darkness seen as unambiguous and absolute evil. Like the German Romantics who influenced him, and indeed like some postmodern thinkers with whom he has been compared, MacDonald resisted absolute dualisms, or binary oppositions.[19] The Shadow acquired by Anodos in the Church of Darkness, after his intrusion into the forbidden cupboard, is a *necessary* Shadow; his fall here is a *felix culpa*. Kristeva, too, in her *Powers of Horror* refers to the *felix culpa* idea in the chapter entitled "Qui tollis peccata mundi." She refers to Duns Scotus's spiritual revolution, which allowed the remission of sin by bringing sin into speech in

---

[18] Johann Wolfgang von Goethe, *Faust, Part One*, trans. David Luke (Oxford and New York: Oxford University Press, 1981), lines 1349–50. Quoted in *Phantastes*, p. 67.

[19] See Stephen Prickett, "Fictions and Metafictions: 'Phantastes,' 'Wilhelm Meister,' and the idea of the 'Bildungsroman,'" in William Raeper (ed.), *The Gold Thread*, pp. 109–25; Roderick McGillis, Introduction to MacDonald's *The Princess and the Goblin*, and *The Princess and Curdie* (Oxford: Oxford University Press, 1990), pp. vii–xxviii, xvi. On MacDonald's resistance to binary thinking see also Roderick McGillis "*Phantastes and Lilith:* Femininity and Freedom" in *The Gold Thread*, pp. 31–55.

confession and absolution: "It is owing to speech, at any rate, that the lapse has a chance of becoming fortunate: *felix culpa* is merely a phenomenon of enunciation."[20] Underlying Kristeva's theological point is a psychoanalytical one: to acquire a subject position in language or in the symbolic order, requires a breaking loose from, and a rejection of, the abject, ultimately the mother. Therefore the fault that is necessary and ultimately blessed is matricide, for matricide is the condition of the possibility of subjectivity and speech. Kristeva writes provocatively in *Black Sun*: "Matricide is our vital necessity, the sine-qua-non of our individuation." (*BS* 27–8)

But this fall, fault, rejection, and loss have to be *felt* as fall, fault, rejection, and loss, and consequently there occurs mourning, melancholia, and abjection. As Kristeva puts in *Black Sun*: "The child king becomes irredeemably sad before uttering his first words; this is because he has been irrevocably, desperately separated from the mother, a loss that causes him to try to find her again, along with other objects of love, first in the imagination, then in words." (*BS* 6) So if *Phantastes* ends in hope, as Anodos hears the following words in, and permeated by, the semiotic music of the rustling beech leaves: "A great good is coming—is coming—is coming to thee, Anodos" (*Ph* 237), such hope is only bought at the price of *really going through* the guilt and mourning of the so-called "depressive position" of Klein, Winnicott, and Kristeva. Night may ultimately be transfigured, as in Novalis; evil may in the end turn out be, as in Goethe, merely a rather serious joke; but in the meantime the Shadow, with all its distorting and blighting effects, has to be lived with. In a passage that strikingly echoes Nerval, and anticipates Kristeva, Anodos says of his Shadow: "it began to coruscate, and shoot out on all sides a radiation of dim shadow. These rays of gloom issued from the central shadow as from a black sun, lengthening and shortening with continual change. But wherever a ray struck, that part of earth, or sea, or sky, became void and desert, and sad to my heart . . . one ray shot out beyond the rest, seeming to lengthen infinitely, until it smote the great sun on the face, which withered and darkened beneath the blow." (*Ph* 73)

One of the baleful influences of Anodos's "evil demon" is that it disrupts his ability to offer a connected account of his experiences (*Ph* 73). He says: "From this time until I arrived at the palace of Fairy Land, I can attempt no consecutive account of my wanderings and adventures. Everything, henceforward, existed for me in its relation to my attendant." (*Ph* 72) This lack of a consecutive account not only follows Novalis's

---

[20] Kristeva, *Powers of Horror*, p. 131.

description of the *Märchen*, given in the epigraph to the whole novel[21]; it is also, according to Kristeva, related to melancholia. Whether it results from "an inversion of aggressiveness" or from some other cause, "the phenomenon that might be described as a *breakdown of biological and logical sequentiality* finds its radical manifestation in melancholia" (*BS* 20). What Kristeva calls "shattered concatenation" or simply "non-concatenation" is for her a result of the failure to mourn successfully the archaic maternal pre-object, "the Thing." She writes later in *Black Sun*: "From the analyst's point of view, the possibility of concatenating signifiers (words or actions) appears to depend upon going through mourning for an archaic and indispensable object… Mourning for the Thing—such a possibility comes out of transposing, beyond loss and on an imaginary or symbolic level, the imprints of an interchange with the other articulated according to a certain order." (*BS* 40)

More simply put: "If I did not agree to lose mother, I could neither imagine nor name her." (*BS* 41) It is significant that Anodos says that his inability to give a consecutive account of his wanderings lasts until he arrives at the palace of Fairy Land (*Ph* 72). Anodos's stay in the palace is at the centre of *Phantastes*, and central to his time there are the hours spent reading in the marvellous palace library. Reading in this library is a magical experience. Anodos finds that his identity is taken over by the text; he *becomes* the text, or conversely, the text gives him an identity. One of the stories he reads forms the central chapter of *Phantastes*. This story is a Hoffmannesque tale within a tale about Cosmo von Wehrstahl, a student in Prague, though of course as Anodos says: "while I read it, I was Cosmo, and his history was mine. Yet, all the time, I seemed to have a kind of double-consciousness, and the story a double meaning." (*Ph* 106) Cosmo/Anodos/the reader—for as Stephen Prickett says, this *Bildungsroman* is above all about the formation of the *reader*[22]—acquires a magic mirror in which he discovers in his *reflected* room a beautiful woman with whom he falls obsessively in love. The tale is about Cosmo's quest to be united with the object of his longing desire, which he only achieves in the end at the cost of his own death, after having smashed the

---

[21] "A *Märchen* is like a dream image without coherence … In a genuine *Märchen* everything must be miraculous, mysterious and incoherent … here begins the time of anarchy, of lawlessness, freedom … the world of the *Märchen* is a total opposition to the world of truth and for that very reason has the total likeness to it that chaos has to the completed creation." In MacDonald's text the epigraph is untranslated; the translation here is mine. On the history of omissions and misprints relating to these Novalis extracts see Wolff, *The Golden Key*, pp. 42–5.
[22] Prickett, op. cit., in Raeper (ed.), *The Gold Thread*, p 117.

mirror. That the centre of this *Bildungsroman* should be occupied by a tale about a magic mirror, which is explicitly compared with the imagination (*Ph* 112–3), invites reference to Lacan's "mirror stage" and "the imaginary." Yet more interesting from Kristeva's point of view is the way that here the concept of identity, union with the loved object, and a death bordering on suicide come together in a kind of *jouissance*. This mutual interplay of the themes of identity, love, the maternal, and death by suicide, dominates the remainder of *Phantastes*.

After the mirror episode, in a scene that reverses the ending of Novalis's *Märchen* "Hyacinth and Roseblossom", Anodos finally unveils his Isis only to have her writhe from his arms and disappear, leaving him desolate. He continues his journey "with a dull endurance, varied by moments of uncontrollable sadness" and comes to a bleak shoreline, "bare and waste, and gray" (*Ph* 157; 159). The following powerful evocation of desolation and despair, which one critic thinks may be in part a response to Arnold's "Dover Beach," seen in manuscript form,[23] culminates in the simple statement: "I could bear it no longer." (*Ph* 159) Anodos throws himself into the sea: "I stood one moment and gazed into the heaving abyss beneath me; then plunged headlong … A blessing, like the kiss of a mother, seemed to alight on my soul; a calm, deeper than that which accompanies a hope deferred, bathed my spirit. I sank far into the waters, and sought not to return. I felt as if once more the great arms of the beech-tree were around me, soothing me after the miseries I had passed through, and telling me, like a little sick child, that I should be better tomorrow." (*Ph* 160)

Saved by a little boat that miraculously appears, Anodos lies in a trance: "In dreams of unspeakable joy … I passed through [a] wondrous twilight. I awoke with the feeling that I had been kissed and loved to my heart's content." (*Ph* 161–2) Kristeva's comment in *Black Sun* seems remarkably apt at this point: "One can imagine the delights of reunion that a regressive daydream promises itself through the nuptials of suicide." (*BS* 14) It is as if Anodos is plunging from the unbearable symbolic order back into the sweet annihilation of self in the primal chaos that Kristeva associates with suicide: "The depressive denial that destroys the meaning of the symbolic also destroys the act's meaning, and leads the subject to commit suicide without anguish of disintegration, as a reuniting with archaic non-integration, as lethal as it is jubilatory, 'oceanic.'" (*BS* 19)

---

[23] David S. Robb, *George MacDonald* (Edinburgh: Scottish Academic Press, 1987) pp. 80–3.

Suicide is the way back to "the non integrated self's lost paradise, one without others or limits, a fantasy of untouchable fullness" (*BS* 20). And it is quite fitting that Anodos's way should now take him back to the most explicitly maternal figure in the book, the wise old woman with young eyes who lives in a magic cottage. It is fitting because, according to Kristeva, the act of suicide is a way of avoiding matricide, which is, as we have seen, "our vital necessity, the sine-qua-non condition of our individuation" (*BS* 27–8). She writes in the same passage in *Black Sun*: "The lesser or greater violence of matricidal drive . . . entails, when it is hindered, its inversion on the self: the maternal object having been introjected, the depressive or melancholic putting to death of the self is what follows, instead of matricide. In order to protect mother I kill myself." (*BS* 28) Having killed himself, Anodos has saved his all-providing mother: "While she sung, I was in Elysium ... I felt as if she could give me everything I wanted; as if I should never wish to leave her, but would be content to be sung to and fed by her, day after day, as years rolled by." (*Ph* 171) Anodos does nevertheless attempt to leave her by going through each of the four doors in the cottage, but returns each time after having encountered, respectively: the death of his brother; the disappearance of the Knight and his lady behind an obviously parental bedroom door; a dead lover and/or mother; and whatever lay behind the fourth door, which he cannot bring to consciousness. In other words, behind each door lies obviously oedipal material which Anodos cannot face; he must return to "the floor of the cottage, with my head in the lap of the woman, who was weeping over me, and stroking my hair with both hands, talking to me as a mother might talk to a sick and sleeping, or a dead child." (*Ph* 182) However, the old woman finally persuades Anodos to leave, gently pushing him away with the words "Go, my son, and do something worth doing." The last sentence of this chapter reads: "I felt very desolate as I went." (*Ph* 184)

Nevertheless, in the next section Anodos does do something worth doing. He teams up with two brothers in order to kill three giants who have been terrorizing the countryside, and is fêted as the conquering hero in the court of the grateful king, whose two sons died in defeating the giants. Superficially, then, Anodos seems to have successfully entered the symbolic order; but he is still haunted by the Shadow. As he enters an enchanted wood, the Shadow suddenly disappears. Anodos becomes euphoric and begins to develop an inflated sense of self, until he encounters a more powerful *Doppelgänger* who totally deflates his sense of self-worth, and leads him, cowed, to a "dreary square tower" in which he is imprisoned with his Shadow, which has meanwhile reappeared (*Ph*

205). Again, Kristeva's version of psychoanalysis seems to fit MacDonald's text uncannily well. In her discussion of borderline cases in *Powers of Horror* she calls this kind of patient a "fortified castle," and writes:

> Constructed on the one hand by the incestuous desire of (for) his   mother and on the other by an overly brutal separation from her, the borderline patient, even though he may be a fortified castle, is nevertheless an empty castle. The absence, or the failure, of paternal function to establish a unitary bent between subject and object, produces this strange configuration: an encompassment that is stifling ... and, at the same time, draining. The ego then plunges into a pursuit of identifications that could repair narcissism—identifications that the subject will experience as insignificant, "empty", "null", "devitalized" and "puppet-like". An empty castle, haunted by unappealing ghosts—"powerless" outside, "impossible" inside.[24]

But not for the first time, Anodos is liberated by the semiotic: a song enters his prison-house: "it bathed me like a sea; inwrapt me like an odorous vapour; entered my soul like a long draught of clear spring-water; shone upon me like essential sunlight; soothed me like a mother's voice and hand." (*Ph* 208) Anodos is able now simply to walk out the door of the castle, where he finds the singer, a beautiful woman whose magic globe he had shattered long before, just after he had acquired his Shadow. The woman has, through the power of the Fairy Queen, become a wandering agent of liberation, delivering people by the power of her song. Anodos can now give up his "vain attempt to behold, if not my ideal in myself, at least myself in my ideal" (*Ph* 212); that is, perhaps, the vain pursuit of "insignificant" identifications that would repair narcissism (to use Kristeva's terms). He experiences what Kristeva says we are all ultimately looking for, and especially in psychoanalysis—a new birth: "Another self seemed to arise like a white spirit from a dead man, from the dumb and trampled self of the past. Doubtless, this self must again die and be buried and again from its tomb spring a winged child ... Self will come to life even in the slaying of self." (*Ph* 212)[25]

---

[24] Kristeva, *Powers of Horror*, pp. 48–9.
[25] Cf. Novalis's concept of *Selbsttödtung* (which Thomas Carlyle translates as "annihilation of self"), and which MacDonald would have known from Carlyle's essay on Novalis if not from Novalis himself. See Thomas Carlyle, "Novalis" in *Critical and Miscellaneous Essays*, vol. 2 (London: Chapman and Hall, 1899), pp. 1–55.

Underway again, Anodos once more hears a voice singing, but this time a manly voice. It is the Knight, dragging behind his horse the hideous corpse of a dragon, described in lurid detail, surely an instance of the abject. However the conquering Knight is hardly the stern oedipal father figure one might perhaps anticipate; rather his feminine qualities are stressed. He has "all the gentleness of a womanly heart"(*Ph* 216); he tends to a wounded child "if possible even more gently than the mother" (*Ph* 217). Anodos begs to become the Knight's squire, and although this could be read in straightforwardly oedipal terms, the Knight has enough of the maternal and the semiotic about him to suggest that he is perhaps rather the *Black Sun*'s pre-oedipal "father in individual prehistory"(*BS* 13), "primary identification" with whom allows reconciliation with loss of "the Thing." Such reconciliation, which allows the transition from the pre-symbolic (or pre-object-choice) stage into the symbolic order, is very much the province of religion. As Kristeva says in *Powers of Horror*: "it is within that undecidable space, logically coming before the choice of the sexual object, that the religious answer to abjection breaks in: *defilement, taboo*, or *sin*."[26] Or *sacrifice*, Kristeva might have added at this point.[27] And indeed it is to a strange religious ceremony that the Knight leads Anodos, where they witness a ritual human sacrifice, in which the victims are devoured by being pushed into a door in a great pedestal supporting an enthroned image. The Knight seems to acquiesce in all this, but Anodos does not. In a violent gesture which resists the institutionalized violence of the sacrifice which founds the symbolic order, he strides up to the image, overthrows it and grapples with the beast which emerges from the gaping hole under the displaced image. Though he dies in its embrace (and there is a strong suggestion of suicide), Anodos manages to kill the devouring monster. One suspects that although he seems finally to have managed to kill his mother, by dying himself he has achieved ultimate union or identification with her in a state which seems as much pre-natal as post-mortem: "Now that I lay in her bosom, the whole earth, and each of her births, was as a body to me, at my will. I seemed to feel the great heart of the mother beating into mine, and feeding me with her own life, her own essential being and nature." (*Ph* 232)

Anodos enjoys not being. The following (and penultimate) chapter begins: "I was dead, and right content." (*Ph* 230) There follows an at times sentimental, at times didactic, and at times bizarre evocation of "a state of

---

[26] Kristeva, *Powers of Horror*, p. 48.
[27] For Kristeva on sacrifice, see John Lechte, *Julia Kristeva* (London: Routledge, 1990), pp. 73–5, 148–9; also Kelly Oliver, *Reading Kristeva: Unraveling the Double-bind* (Bloomington: Indiana University Press, 1993), pp. 40–1.

ideal bliss" with echoes of Plato, Novalis, Goethe, and William Blake, and the suggestion of an identification of Anodos with Christ himself (*Ph* 234). From this "state of ideal bliss" Anodos is wrenched: "a pang and a terrible shudder went through me; a writhing as of death convulsed me; and I became once again conscious of a more limited, even a bodily and earthly life." (*Ph* 233) Paradoxically, it is a death agony that brings Anodos back to *this* life, a life that "seemed to correspond to what we think death is, before we die." (*Ph* 234) There is also a strong suggestion of *jouissance,* a violent "coming" into contact with "the real." And in a literal sense, Anodos has come home, back to quotidian reality.

Yet what constitutes "the real" is precisely the issue which remains undecided at the end of *Phantastes*. On one level there is the theme, typical of German Romanticism, of a banal common life that needs somehow to be synthesized with the free play of fantasy. But MacDonald at the end of his novel backs off from the radically Utopian vision whose traces haunt the margins of the Novalis quotations which preface *Phantastes*. The promised "great good coming" to Anodos (*Ph* 237) is not the radical poeticization of reality projected by Novalis's "magic idealism". Despite its semiotic trappings, the promise seems to amount to little more than the platitudinous: "what we call evil, is the only and best shape, which, for the person and his condition at the time, could be assumed by the best good." (*Ph* 237) And if MacDonald fails to follow through the dialectic of Novalis, it might equally be said that he fails to follow through Kristeva's dialectic of the semiotic and the symbolic. The consequent precariousness of the subject-position achieved at the end of *Phantastes* is confirmed by MacDonald's later fantasy work *Lilith,* where things start to fall apart in a spectacular and disturbing way.[28] The question remains of course as to whether the projects of personal and social transformation in the writings of Novalis and Kristeva are in reality more than desperate attempts by what Kelly Oliver calls "melancholy theoreticians" to come to terms with profound feelings of personal loss through the practice of writing.[29] Perhaps the modest, ambiguous ending of *Phantastes* is not without a certain courage, the "corage" to which George MacDonald aspired when he took as his motto the anagram of his name "Corage: God mend al." That courage is in the first place "the courage to be" or to use Kristeva's terms in *Black Sun*, the resistance to the "*I AM THAT WHICH IS NOT*". (*BS* 146)

---

[28] George MacDonald, *Lilith* [1895] (Grand Rapids: Eerdmans, 1981).
[29] Oliver, op. cit., p. 143.

CHAPTER TWO

THE ANGEL IN THE HOUSE OF DEATH:
GENDER AND SUBJECTIVITY
IN GEORGE MACDONALD'S *LILITH*

This chapter explores the representation of the female (and specifically the maternal) in *Lilith,* the fantasy novel by George MacDonald. The pertinence of such an exploration to the theme of the "Angel in the House"[1] is confirmed by Barbara Koltuv in *The Book of Lilith* when, in the chapter entitled "Lilith and the Daughters of Eve", she cites *in extenso* the passage in Virginia Woolf's essay "Professions for Women" which emphasizes the need to kill the Angel in the House.[2] Koltuv is a Jungian analyst who talks of "the war between Eve and Lilith", or in less oppositional language "the [endless] cycle of alterations between the Lilith and Eve aspects of woman's psyche".[3] Another Jungian analyst, Siegmund Hurwitz, has taken Koltuv to task in his *Lilith: The First Eve,* ostensibly for scholarly inadequacies, but by implication as one of those who overlook the point that the Lilith material is "above all about the anima problem of the Jewish male", and "only applies externally ... to the real woman in a secondary fashion".[4] While I personally retain a degree of agnosticism about the Jungian *gnosis,* I find it difficult to resist the analogy that George MacDonald's *Lilith* is about the problem (call it "anima problem" if you will) of a *Scottish* male. However, there seems something sexist in Hurwitz's assumption that male images of women

---

[1] The original context of this paper was a conference, and subsequent collection of essays, on the theme *Women of Faith in Victorian Culture: reassessing 'The Angel in the House'*. For publication details see the Acknowledgements section above.
[2] See Virginia Woolf, "Professions for Women" in Stephen Greenblatt and M.H. Abrams (eds), *The Norton Anthology of English Literature* Vol. 2 (Eighth Edition) (New York: W.W. Norton, 2006), p. 2153.
[3] Barbara Koltuv, *The Book of Lilith* (York Beach, Maine: Nicholas-Hays, 1986), p. 83.
[4] Siegmund Hurwitz, *Lilith: The First Eve* (Einsiedeln: Daimon Verlag, 1992), p. 12.

only apply "externally in a secondary fashion" to "the real woman". Surely the point of much feminist writing has been that male images generated by male problems have been foisted (no doubt "in a secondary fashion") onto women to such an extent that sometimes "the real woman" has been hard to find? There are of course different feminist responses to this situation. One such response arguably relevant to George MacDonald's work is that of Lynne Pearce in her book *Woman/Image/Text,* where she raises the question of whether reading Pre-Raphaelite art and literature "against the grain" can in some cases only ever be a Pyrrhic victory.[5] The works in question leave so little space for a feminist reading that the game is simply not worth the candle. Whether MacDonald's work falls into this category remains to be seen. Another response, feminist perhaps only "under erasure", is that of Julia Kristeva. Kristeva's writings are both provocative and suggestive from a psychoanalytical point of view, and what she does for example in "Stabat Mater"[6] seems to offer a fruitful way of exploring patriarchal images and fantasies of "women". The approach she develops in her texts of the 1980s *(Powers of Horror, Tales of Love* and *Black Sun*[7]) seems to work particularly well with George MacDonald's fantasy writing. Returning to the Angel in the House (whose murder Virginia Woolf proposed), an opposition is set up by Kultov between the wild and murderous Lilith and the nurturing Mother Eve[8]. Kultov does not explicitly identify Eve with the Angel in the House, but there can be little doubt that they are closely associated if not identified. There is a strong suggestion that in a sense it is Mother Eve (the Eve of patriarchal construction) who needs to be killed for women to achieve freedom and dignity. In Kristeva's terms, the need for such matricide in the symbolic order is related in a complex way to the more primal need for the matricide which is, as she controversially puts it in *Black Sun:* "our vital necessity, the sine-qua-non condition of our individuation ..."[9] For Kristeva, individuation as such demands the leaving, the losing, symbolically the killing, of the original all-embracing Mother or the *chora.* Failure to "kill

[5] Lynne Pearce, *Woman/Image/Text* (London: Harvester Wheatsheaf, 1991), p. 139.
[6] Toril Moi (ed.), *The Kristeva Reader* (Oxford: Blackwell, 1986), pp. 160-186; also in Julia Kristeva [1983] *Tales of Love* (New York: Columbia University Press, 1987).
[7] Julia Kristeva, *Powers of Horror: An Essay on Abjection* [1980] (New York: Columbia University Press, 1982); *Tales of Love* (see previous note); *Black Sun: Depression and Melancholy*[1987] (New York Columbia University Press, 1989).
[8] Kultov, loc. cit.
[9] Kristeva, *Black Sun,* p. 27f.

the mother" can result ultimately only in psychosis or suicide, according to Kristeva. Matricide in this sense is literally a case of murder in self-defence.

George MacDonald's fantasy writing is transparently all about the Mother, as R.L. Wolff[10] and David Holbrook'[11] in their different ways have shown. More specifically, as I have tried to show elsewhere,[12] MacDonald's fantasy writing is about the dilemma of losing or killing or taking leave of the Mother in order to be somebody *or* holding fast to the Mother, but at the price of not being somebody, that is, in psychosis or suicide. There is biographical evidence which suggests that the melancholy which pervades MacDonald's writing goes back to a traumatic primary experience with his mother[13]; but in any case the texts themselves witness to an intense struggle with the figure of the Mother, a struggle literally to the death. This struggle is nowhere more evident than in his last major work *Lilith,* published in 1895, when MacDonald was aged seventy-one. There are many similarities between *Lilith* and *Phantastes,* MacDonald's other fantasy novel, published nearly forty years previously.

Both novels are dominated by a tension between various incarnations, on the one hand, of the Angel in the House (in *Phantastes* this is above all the wise old woman with young eyes in the magic cottage), and on the other of a female demon (in *Phantastes* this is the ogre in "the Church of Darkness", but above all the Alder-maiden, who, like Lilith, "will smother you with her web of hair, if you let her near you at night"[14]). The "Shadow" also figures in both novels, though much more prominently in *Phantastes*, where the plot mostly revolves around Anodos's attempts to become free of his "Shadow", the depression or melancholy that afflicts him. In *Lilith* the "Shadow" is in a sense much more objectively, if

---

[10] Robert Lee Wolff, *The Golden Key: A Study of the Fiction of George MacDonald* (New Haven: Yale University Press, 1961).

[11] George MacDonald, *Phantastes,* with an Introduction by David Holbrook (London: Everyman Paperback, 1983). Holbrook subsequently published *A Study of George Macdonald and the Image of Woman* (New York: Edwin Mellen, 2000).

[12] See Chapter One above, "George MacDonald, Julia Kristeva and the Black Sun".

[13] In a secret drawer in MacDonald's desk were found, after his death, a lock of his mother's hair and a letter by her containing the following reference to his premature weaning, 'I cannot help in my heart being very much grieved for him yet, for he has not forgot it ... he cryed desperate for a while in the first night, but he has cryed very little since and I hope the worst is over now'; see Greville MacDonald, *George MacDonald and His Wife* (London: George Allen and Unwin, 1924), p. 32

[14] George MacDonald, *Phantastes* (London: Dent Everyman, 1915), p. 10.

intermittently, present as the consort of Lilith, and is even referred to as Samoil, presumably a corruption of Samael, the Satan of the Kabbalah. In contrast, in *Phantastes* the threat of the female demon is certainly present, but it does not dominate the novel in the way that it does in *Lilith*. *Phantastes* is clearly a *Bildungsroman,* concerned with the formation of the young hero (and the writer—and also perhaps the reader[15]). However, although the narrator of *Lilith* is also a young man, the novel is not so much about his formation as it is about the part he plays in a much larger and age-old drama which culminates the overcoming and "redemption" of Lilith. *Lilith* is certainly a psychological novel, but it is also a mythological as well as a theological one.

Lilith is above all about two competing images or constructions of "woman": Lilith versus Eve. It is only gradually revealed to the reader that Mr and Mrs Raven are Adam and Eve. But already on his first meeting with Mrs Raven, the narrator, Vane, has a numinous experience:

> The sexton [Mr Raven] said something to his wife that made her turn towards us. —What a change had passed upon her! It was as if the splendour of her eyes had grown too much for them to hold, and, sinking into her countenance, made it flash with a loveliness like that of Beatrice in the white rose of the redeemed.
>
> Life itself, life eternal, immortal, streamed from it, an unbroken lightning. Even her hands shone with a white radiance, every "pearl-shell helmet" gleaming like a moonstone. Her beauty was overpowering; I was glad when she turned it from me.[16]

The narrator's first encounter with Lilith (as yet unnamed) is also numinous:

> Then I saw, slowly walking over the light soil, the form of a woman ... She was beautiful, but with such a pride at once and misery on her countenance that I could hardly believe what yet I saw. Up and down she walked, vainly endeavouring to lay hold of the mist and wrap it around her. The eyes in the beautiful face were dead, and on her left side was a dark spot, against which she would now and then press her hand, as if to stifle pain or sickness. Her hair hung nearly to her feet, and sometimes the wind would so mix it with the mist that I could not distinguish the one from the other, but when it fell gathering together again, it shone a pale gold in the

---

[15] See Stephen Prickett, "Fictions and Metafictions: 'Phantastes,' 'Wilhelm Meister,' and the idea of the 'Bildungsroman,'" in William Raeper (ed.), *The Gold Thread* (Edinburgh: Edinburgh University Press, 1990), p 117.
[16] George MacDonald, *Lilith* (Grand Rapids: Eerdmans, 1981), p.32. Hereafter cited in parentheses as *L*.

moonlight. Suddenly pressing both hands on her heart, she fell to the ground, and the mist rose from her and melted in the air. I ran to her. But she began to writhe in such torture that I stood aghast. A moment more and her legs, hurrying from her body, sped away serpents. From her shoulders fled her arms as in terror, serpents also. Then something flew up from her like a bat, and when I looked again, she was gone. The ground rose like the sea in a storm; terror laid hold upon me; I turned to the hills and ran. (*L* 50)

Eve and Lilith seem to represent binary opposites: immortal life versus sickness, pain and death; presence and plenitude versus disintegration and dispersal; the power of the gaze versus vulnerability to the gaze; and above all (echoing Woolf's 'Angel of the House' passage) purity versus impurity. And yet each of these opposites is dangerous: the sacred and the taboo; the sublime and the abject; the perfectly self-same and the threateningly other; each seems to derive from a place which is uncanny and unfit for human life. Perhaps MacDonald's Eve and Lilith, split apart as they are, can only offer suicide or psychosis as the consequence of not successfully negotiating a break with the maternal body or *chora* in order to become somebody else.

Vane has a further glimpse of the as yet unnamed Lilith as a woman in "the evil wood" urging on a "strife-tormented multitude" in a furious battle. (*L* 54) A little later he hears Mara's version of the story of the evil princess (Mara is the daughter of Eve, and very much identified with her mother). Lilith herself first confronts him as what seems to be a corpse or a skeleton: "a body it was however, and no skeleton, though as nearly one as body could well be." (*L* 96) The naked, ghastly form seems very much to represent what Kristeva calls the "abject", that is, the maternal body become a phobic object.[17] Technically the "abject" is not an "object" at all, however, because it comes from the place that is prior to the split between subject and object, between "self" and "other", which happens in the symbolic order. The abject is the "other" which is not yet properly distinguished from the self; it is the outside which is not yet properly distinguished from the inside, and is therefore threatening to the precarious emergent self. The "abject" is the improper, the unclean: filth, waste (out of which Lilith, according to one Jewish tradition, was formed).[18] It is the corpse, and especially, as here, a corpse that is "alive": the living dead. It is no surprise that Lilith turns out to be a vampire. And yet not only will

---

[17] Cf. Kelly Oliver, *Reading Kristeva: Unraveling the Double-bind* (Bloomington: Indiana University Press, 1993), p. 58.
[18] Cf. Koltuv, op. cit., p. 19.

Vane not abandon this repulsive female body; in a disturbingly necrophiliac gesture he goes to bed with this quasi-corpse:

> I crept into the heap of leaves, got as dose to her as I could, and took her in my arms. I had not much heat left in me, but what I had I would share with her. Thus I spent what remained of the night ... Her cold seemed to radiate into me, but no heat to pass from me to her. (*L* 97)

In the three months Vane spends trying to resuscitate the corpse, he spends much time washing her (perhaps a case of the ritual purification of the taboo?), and trying to feed her. He dreams of her transformation into Eve:

> Every time I slept, I dreamed of finding a wounded angel, who, unable to fly, remained with me until at last she loved me and would not leave me; and every time I woke, it was to see, instead of an angel-visage with lustrous eyes, the white motionless, wasted face upon the couch. (*L* 102)

Yet ironically it is only when he is asleep that Lilith feeds off him, sucking his blood in the form of a great white leech. In psychoanalytical terms, this is surely a classic tale of the "biter bit". The anxiety and aggression involved in devouring the mother are projected on to the maternal figure in a situation where mother and infant are not yet dearly sorted out. And yet having preserved this repulsive yet fascinating female figure by unknowingly giving his blood, Vane is himself literally repulsed by her. She leaves him, yet:

> I followed her like a child whose mother pretends to abandon him. "I will be your slave!" I said, and laid my head on her arm. She turned as if a serpent had bit her. I cowered before the blaze of her eyes, but could not avert my own. (*L* 110)

His dreams of finding an angel who will not leave him having been shattered, Vane nevertheless continues to pursue Lilith. At length, utterly exhausted, she lies down and takes him in her arms:

> Suddenly [her arms] closed about my neck, rigid as those of the torture-maiden. She drew down my face to hers, and her lips clung to my cheek. A sting of pain shot somewhere through me, and pulsed. I could not stir a hair's breadth. Gradually the pain ceased. A slumberous weariness, a dreamy pleasure stole over me, and then I knew nothing. (*L* 110)

The sexual aspect of his coming together with Lilith is even more explicit later in her palace when he regains consciousness out of a "delicious languor", a floating in sheer pleasure, a dying. He finds Lilith, wearing "a look of satisfied passion", above him (*L* 132-3), a position that of course Adam would not stand for, though MacDonald does not make this point overtly. But at this stage in the narrative Lilith has had enough of Vane; she changes into a leopard, and speeds off to her palace.

It is there that Vane eventually catches up with Lilith, and before she comes to his bed, she gives her version of her story. Lilith's version is presented as mendacious; however one passage does ring true to the character of Lilith as revealed later. She says: "I knew that, if you saw me as I am, you would love me—like the rest of them—to have and to hold. I would none of that either! I would be otherwise loved!" (*L* 130) Despite the humiliation and virtual castration that Lilith will have to undergo at the hands of Adam, Eve and the family, this cry rings strongly from the heart of the novel: "I would be otherwise loved!"

The dramatic confrontation between Lilith and Raven, who finally reveals himself as Adam, occurs after Lilith follows Vane back into "our" world in the form of a Persian cat. Raven reads aloud a poem recounting Lilith's story, which provokes Lilith into revealing herself. Raven then appears as Adam and proceeds to give the "definitive" patriarchal version of Lilith's story. Lilith was an "angelic splendour" brought by God to Adam to be his wife. She however could only think of *power,* and counted it slavery to be one with Adam and bear children (*L* 147). Lilith fled to "the army of the aliens", ensnared the heart of the great Shadow so that he became her slave and made her queen of Hell. According to Adam she is the vilest of God's creatures, living by the blood and lives and souls of men (*L* 148). But then God gave Adam another wife—not an angel but a woman—who is to Lilith as light is to darkness. But there is hope for Lilith, for even she shall be saved by her childbearing (*L* 148). This prophecy wll finally be fulfilled when, through her own death, Lilith's daughter Lona brings about her mother's fall from power (*L* 184-6), a fall which in the patriarchal version naturally constitutes Lilith's "redemption". The story of Lilith's "redemption" might be summarized as follows. Adam calls upon Lilith to repent, but she defies him, saying: "'I will not repent. I will drink the blood of thy child.'" (*L* 149) Adam responds by imprisoning Lilith, but her magic enables her to escape, and she is pursued to her palace by an army of the so-called Little Ones led by Vane and her daughter Lona. When Lona seeks to embrace her mother, she is dashed to the floor and killed. The "murdering princess" is however captured, having reverted to the withered, wasted, corpse-like condition in which Vane first found her (*L* 185). She is carried off in triumph to Adam, but *en route* the victorious army stops at Mara's house, "the House of Bitterness", where Lilith's re-education begins. Asked three times by Mara to repent, Lilith, now a "seeming corpse", answers: "'I will not. I will be myself and not another.'" (L 199) The dialogue continues, with Lilith sounding ever more like an existentialist feminist hero:

> "Alas, you are another now, not yourself! Will you not be your real self?'"
> "I will be what I mean myself now."
> "If you were restored, would you not make what amends you could for the misery you have caused?"
> "I would do after my nature."
> "You do not know it: your nature is good, and you do evil!"
> "I will do as my Self pleases — as my Self desires."
> "You are not the Self you imagine."
> "So long as I feel myself what it pleases me to think myself, I care not. I am content to be to myself what I would be. What I choose to seem to myself makes me what I am. My own thought makes me me; my own thought of myself is me. Another shall not make me!"
> "Such a compulsion would be without value. But there is a light that goes deeper than the will, a light that lights up the darkness behind it: that light can change your will, can make it truly yours and not another's—not the Shadow's. Into the created can pour itself the creating will, and so redeem it!"
> "That light shall not enter me: I hate it! Begone, slave!" (L 199-200)

But the light does enter Lilith, in the form of a "worm-thing … white-hot, vivid as incandescent silver, the live heart of essential fire", which creeps out of the fire to penetrate Lilith: "The Princess gave one writhing, contorted shudder, and ... the worm was in her secret chamber." (L 201)

Despite going through "horror", "torture" and "the hell of self-consciousness" as the central fire of the universe radiates into her, Lilith nevertheless proves very difficult to break. She persists in her defiance, even when visited by "an invisible darkness … a horrible Nothingness, a Negation positive ... Death Absolute ... not the absence of everything, but the presence of Nothing". (L 204) In this quasi-existentialist encounter with Nothingness: "[t]he princess dashed herself ... to the floor with an exceeding great and bitter cry. It was the recoil of Being from Annihilation." (L 204) *Still* Lilith will not submit, until she undergoes "the most fearful thing of all" which is beyond knowledge and even imagination. She goes alone into the outer darkness, into living death, into a dismay beyond misery, a dismay beyond expression. Her face

> sent out a livid gloom, the light that was in her was darkness, and after its kind it shone. She was what God could not have created. She had usurped beyond her share in self-creation, and her part had undone her. She saw now what she had made, and behold, it was not good! (L 206)

If this glimpse "into the heart of horror essential" must in theological terms be a vision of Hell, in psychoanalytical terms it recalls Winnicott's "unthinkable anxiety"[19] located in a place prior to self-hood, let alone knowledge. And "The light that … in her was darkness" recalls the "black sun", the primal unnameable horror, evoked by Kristeva not only in *Black Sun* but also in *Powers of Horror*.[20] Confronted by this horror far beyond mere annihilation, Lilith finally yields and begs to die. She is now ready to be taken to Adam and Eve in the House of Death. Her subjugation is not yet complete, however; the final humiliation is to have to beg to be symbolically castrated by asking Adam to sever her hand, which she cannot open (could the Goethe-loving MacDonald have been unaware that the clenched fist that must be cut off is in German *Faust*?). Using the sword that once guarded the gate of Eden, Adam severs the hand of Lilith, who is now finally allowed to die. Broken by the threat of psychosis, the unnameable horror, Lilith has finally submitted to a fate in which suicide seems to coincide with assimilation into the patriarchal symbolic order, that is, the House of Death.

Eve has triumphed over Lilith. The Angel in the House has not been killed but is as alive and as well as a woman can be in the House of Death. In Kristeva's terms, we might say that matricide has been avoided. The Mother has been preserved, but at the cost of a kind of suicide, what Kristeva calls "the depressive or melancholic putting to death of the self … instead of matricide. In order to protect mother I kill myself …".[21] The suicide in question here is, of course, not only that of Lilith, but also that of George MacDonald, who is clearly "of Lilith's party", perhaps without knowing it. MacDonald's suicide is not literal, but is expressed in the depression which haunted his life from his youth, when he is remembered as repeating "I wis we war a' deid",[22] to the final lapse into five years of silence at the end of his life. The triumph of the Angel in the House represents the defeat not only of a woman who would be "otherwise loved" but also of a man who would love otherwise. In theological terms, *Lilith* also seems to represent the failure of a Christian who would have faith "otherwise". The text is shot through with allusions to Gnostic motifs; but in the end it seems that it is the "martinet God" (as MacDonald

---

[19] D. W. Winnicott, *The Maturational Process and the Facilitating Environment* (London: Hogarth, 1965), p. 57f; and *Home is Where We Start From* (Harmondsworth: Penguin, 1986), p. 32.

[20] Julia Kristeva, *Powers of Horror,* pp. 34ff.

[21] Julia Kristeva, *Black Sun,* p. 28.

[22] Greville MacDonald, *George MacDonald and His Wife* (London: George Allen and Unwin, 1924), p. 84.

once called him[23]) who seems to triumph through his representative Adam and his angels in the house. But the book does not end without hope, if "unconcludedness" can be read as "not without hope"; for the "final" chapter of *Lilith* is entitled "The Endless Ending". At the last moment, Vane is denied access to the throne of the Ancient of Days, and returns to his library, literally uncertain where he is, or whether he is awake or dreaming. Wherever he is, Vane waits, pondering MacDonald's favourite quotation from that great modern Gnostic, Novalis: "Our life is no dream, but it should and will perhaps become one."[24] It is significant that MacDonald's first fantasy novel, *Phantastes,* begins with a lengthy extract from Novalis, and his final fantasy novel ends with a quotation from the same author. To read MacDonald "against the grain" would be to follow his ambivalent but deep-rooted attraction to the radical explorations of Novalis. In the new ways opened up by Novalis[25], moving beyond the deathly double-bind of *either* Eve *or* Lilith, we might perhaps find Sophia.

---

[23] Unspoken Sermons, 3rd Series 161, Quoted in William Raeper, *George MacDonald* (Tring: Lion, 1987) p. 242.

[24] *Lilith* p. 252. Original in Novalis, *Schriften,* ed. Kluckhohn and Samuel, dritter Band (Stuttgart: Kohlhammer, 1960), p. 281.

[25] The name "Novalis" means "one who opens up a new land", according to Margaret Mahoney Stoljar in her Introduction to *Novalis: Philosophical Writings* (trans. and ed by Margaret Mahoney Stoljar) (Albany: SUNY Press, 1997), p. 3.

CHAPTER THREE

STRANGE CASE OF DR MACDONALD AND MR HYDE: ROBERT LOUIS STEVENSON AND GEORGE MACDONALD[1]

Despite the considerable differences in their lives and literary productions, there are nevertheless some intriguing connections between George MacDonald and Robert Louis Stevenson. Although both were Scots, they came from different parts of Scotland, and from different social classes.[2] The specific religious affiliations of their families differed: Stevenson's father was a staunch upholder of the principle of Establishment, while the MacDonalds were in the dissenting Congregationalist tradition. Nevertheless MacDonald and Stevenson both wrestled as young men with religious questions in a broadly similar context (one dominated by various inflections of Calvinism), and both followed paths which, in terms of that shared context, were far from orthodox. Lung problems meant that both writers spent the majority of their life south of Scotland; yet "that grey country, with its rainy sea-beat archipelago," as Stevenson called it,[3] continued to haunt the work of both writers. Both men spent periods convalescing in the Riviera; both tasted, and resisted, celebrity status in the United States of America. And although over the years both have often been consigned (indeed relegated, in terms of the hierarchy of genres in the literary establishment) to the

---

[1] George MacDonald was awarded an honorary LL.D. by his *alma mater*, the University of Aberdeen, in 1868. This essay was originally published as "Amiable Infidelity, Grim-Faced Dummies and Rondels: RLS on George MacDonald" in *North Wind: A Journal of George MacDonald Studies* 23 (2004).

[2] On Stevenson's Scottishness, and especially his relation to the Scottish *Lowlands*, see William Gray, *Robert Louis Stevenson: A Literary Life* (Basingstoke: Palgrave Macmillan, 2004), chapter 3 ('Forever Scotland') *passim*. Stevenson's fascination with the Highlands (about which he planned to write a book) was not based, like MacDonald's, on a direct family connection, though he did fantasise that "Stevenson" was a name adopted by the MacGregors when their name was banned.

[3] The Scot Abroad' in *The Siverado Squatters* (Tusitala Edition vol.18) (London: Heinemann, 1924) pp.172-75.

status of children's writers, both have nevertheless had powerful literary advocates. In MacDonald's case this advocacy came most famously (and as something of a mixed blessing) from C.S. Lewis[4], as well as from W.H. Auden and the early J.R.R. Tolkien[5]; in the case of Stevenson, Graham Greene and Jorge Luis Borges have acknowledged him as their literary master.

The connections between Stevenson and MacDonald which I wish to trace here are not so much references to, or echoes of, Stevenson in the writings of MacDonald, though these may well exist. Rather, I have tracked down references to, and perhaps echoes of, George MacDonald in the writings of Stevenson. Primarily I shall be referring to Stevenson's correspondence, though I believe I have discovered at least one literary echo of MacDonald in one of Stevenson's most famous pieces of fiction.

The first letter by Stevenson referring to MacDonald is to Stevenson's father on 1 September 1868 when Stevenson was seventeen years old. He was staying in Wick in the far north of Scotland, getting some hands-on experience of the family business of engineering; the Stevenson firm was in the process of constructing (abortively, as it turned out) a breakwater for Wick's new harbour. The titanic struggles between the free-thinking young Stevenson and his religiously conservative father were still to come, but perhaps they can be seen looming here as Stevenson tells his father of a Free Church minister in Wick: "Ah fie! What a creed!" the young Stevenson exclaims; "He told me point blank that all Roman Catholics would be damned. I'd rather have MacDonald's amiable infidelity, than this harsh, judging, self-righteous form of faith." He assures his father that he is referring not to the engineer MacDonald who was in charge of the harbour works, but to "George MacDonald, the writer."[6] The seventeen-year-old Stevenson is here doubtless pandering to his father's prejudices in favour of the Established Church in Scotland. Typically, though, while he was willing at this stage to pay lip-service to his father's religious convictions, the young Stevenson was in fact far more interested in people than in intellectual systems; he wrote to his mother a few days later that:

---

[4] On the questionable aspects of Lewis's advocacy of MacDonald, see "Pullman, Lewis, MacDonald and the anxiety of influence" reprinted below.
[5] On Tolkien's later retraction of his earlier enthusiasm for MacDonald, see the chapter on Tolkien in my *Fantasy, Myth and the Measure of Truth* (Palgrave, 2008).
[6] Bradford A. Booth and Ernest Mehew (eds), *The Letters of Robert Louis Stevenson* (in 8 volumes) (New Haven: Yale UP, 1994-5), vol. 1, pp. 139-40. This edition of RLS's Letters is cited hereafter in parentheses as *L 1-8*.

"The Free Church minister and I got quite thick. He left last night about two in the morning". (*L1* 142)

The following June, Stevenson just missed meeting MacDonald in Lerwick. Stevenson was accompanying his father on a tour of inspection to the Orkney and Shetland islands on board the *Pharos*, the official steamer of the Commissioners of Northern Lights. They arrived at Lerwick just a few days after MacDonald had stopped there in the yacht *Blue Bell*, *en route* for Norway. A doctor had had to be called on board to treat MacDonald who was "ill of inflammation of the knee-joint," as Stevenson wrote back to his mother. (*L1* 183) The leeches prescribed by the Lerwick doctor, who passed on this gossip in his "interesting talk" (ibid.) with Stevenson, do not seem to have been very effective. As Greville MacDonald tells us in the chapter entitled "The Blue Bell" in *George MacDonald and His Wife*, MacDonald's condition worsened, so that by the time he arrived back in London via Trondheim and Newcastle, "the emaciated look of my father" led Greville to think that his father was dead.[7] Ironically, while it was a yacht trip taken as a last resort that gave Stevenson the bonus of such life as he was able to enjoy before his early death (the yacht *Casco* figures as Stevenson's "ship of death" through the South Seas[8]), in MacDonald's case a yacht trip was almost the death of him, as Louisa MacDonald wrote in a letter of July 1869. (*GMAW* 395)

The first evidence we have that Stevenson had himself actually read any of MacDonald's works comes over three years later, when he refers to *Phantastes* in a letter to his cousin Bob Stevenson in October 1872.[9] The young RLS was exploring agnosticism—declaiming Walt Whitman, reading Herbert Spencer "very hard," and offering papers to the exclusive Speculative Society, housed in Edinburgh University's Old College, on such topics as "Christ's Teaching and Modern Christianity" and "The Authority of the New Testament". (*L1* 259 and n.13) He had become a member of the so-called L.J.R. Society (standing for Liberty, Justice and Reverence). This was a freethinking offshoot of "the Spec." and met in a bar in Advocate's Close. Its tenets included the abolition of the House of Lords and a freedom from the doctrines of the Established Church; these tenets, and indeed the very existence of the L.J.R., shocked the profoundly

---

[7] Greville MacDonald, *George MacDonald and His Wife* (London: George Allen and Unwin, 1924) [reprinted Johannesen, 1998 p. 394. Hereafter cited in parentheses as *GMAW*.
[8] See William Gray, *Robert Louis Stevenson*, p. 110.
[9] While the previous two references to MacDonald are indexed in volume 1 of the Booth and Mehew edition of the *Letters of Robert Louis Stevenson*, the normally scrupulous Ernest Mehew has omitted this important reference from the index.

conservative Thomas Stevenson. As Stevenson and Charles Baxter were to recall in their correspondence almost twenty years later, there had been hell to pay when Thomas Stevenson had discovered the L.J.R. constitution, probably in the early months of 1873. (*LI* 192 n.6; *L1* 273 n.1) In February 1873, RLS wrote to Baxter: "My dear Baxter, The thunderbolt has fallen with a vengeance now. You know the aspect of a house in which somebody is awaiting burial—the quiet step—the hushed voices and rare conversation—the religious literature that holds a temporary monopoly—the grim, wretched faces; all is here reproduced in this family circle in honour of my (what is it?) atheism or blasphemy." (*L1* 273) It was in the context of this developing religious crisis in the Stevenson household that in October 1872 RLS wrote desperately to his cousin Bob. When accused by Thomas Stevenson of causing Louis to lose his faith, Bob had replied with some sarcasm "that he didn't know where [Louis] had found out that the Christian religion was not true, but that *he* hadn't told [him]". (*L1* 295) If Bob Stevenson was noted for the outrageousness and wit of his talk (W.E. Henley—who knew both men—placed him above Oscar Wilde in this respect), Bob's younger cousin Louis was much more serious about the importance of being earnest. In this letter to Bob, who figures as a mentor, RLS writes:

> My dear Bob, A lot of waves and counter-waves have been beating upon me of late, as this new creed of mine is not ballasted as yet with many Articles, it has tossed terribly about and made my heart sick within me.— There are a sight of hitches not yet disentangled in this Christian skein … One does get so *mixed* - my ears begin to sing, when I think of all that can be said on either side; and I do feel just now that hopeless emptiness about the stomach and desire to sit down and cry … It is all very well to talk about flesh and lusts and such like; but the real hot sweat must come out in this business, or we go alone to the end of life. *I* want an object, a mission, a belief, a hope to be my wife; and, please God, have it I shall. (*L1* 254)

When the twenty-one-year old Stevenson, a rebel without a cause, but desperately in search of *something* to believe in, goes on to refer to *Phantastes*, it is precisely to chapter 23 where the twenty-one year old Anodos (one translation of whose name is of course "pathless") decides to offer himself as squire to the knight. The latter accepts Anodos and offers him the much-needed hand of friendship[10]. The dialogue between Anodos and the knight develops in a vein very similar to that between the young

---

[10] George MacDonald, *Phantastes: A Faërie Romance for Men and Women* [1858] (London: Dent Everyman, 1915), p. 295. Subsequent references are to this edition and will be cited as *Ph* parenthetically in the text

RLS and his older cousin. The knight counsels Anodos that it is sufficient if a man "will settle it with himself, that even renown and success are in themselves of no great value, and be content to be defeated, if so be that the fault is not his" (*Ph* 298-9). The knight's advice must have struck home to the young RLS who four years earlier had confessed to his cousin Bob: "Strange how my mind runs on this idea. Becoming great, becoming great, becoming great. A heart burned out with the lust of this world's approbation: a hideous disease to have." (*L1* 143) Anodos then enquires about the little beggar-girl whom the knight had helped, which prompts the knight's tale of the little girl begging butterflies for wings in order to fly to the country she came from. The terrorization of this little girl by great effigies "made of wood, without knee or elbow-joints, and without any noses or mouths or eyes in their faces" (*Ph* 300), and the knight's vain attempts to destroy them by cutting them to pieces, is what remained in Stevenson's imagination: it surfaces in this letter to Bob when he writes:

> Here is another terrible complaint I bring against our country. I try to learn the truth, and their grim-faced dummies, their wooden effigies and creeds dead years ago at heart, come round me, like the wooden men in *Phantastes*, and I may cut at them and prove them faulty and mortal, but yet they can stamp the life out of me. (*L1* 255)

Stevenson's allusion to this chapter of *Phantastes* in his outcry against the religious oppression he felt he experienced in his native country is apt, in that the chapter goes on to describe Anodos's encounter with corrupt religious ritual.

However, there is another fascinating, and to the best of my knowledge hitherto undetected, echo of this scene in *Phantastes* where wooden monsters seek to trample the little beggar-girl. This echo comes in Stevenson's most celebrated work, *Strange Case of Dr Jekyll and Mr Hyde*, published more than a decade after the letter to Bob containing the *Phantastes* reference, and famously based on a dream which was written up in circumstances almost as well-known as the story itself.[11] The opening sequence of *Jekyll and Hyde* is dominated by the image of the creature (who we will later discover is Henry Jekyll's *alter ego* Mr Hyde) trampling on a little girl: "the man trampled calmly over the child's body and left her screaming on the ground. It sounds nothing to hear, but it was hellish to see. It wasn't like a man; it was like some damned Juggernaut."[12]

---

[11] On the twists and turns of the myth about the writing of *Strange Case of Dr Jekyll and Mr Hyde*, see William Gray, *Robert Louis Stevenson*, p. 176, note 15.
[12] *The Strange Case of Dr Jekyll and Mr Hyde; Fables* [1886] (Tusitala Edition vol.5) (London: Heinemann, 1924), p. 3.

In his essay "A Chapter on Dreams" Stevenson divides the labour of his literary production (of his creative work in general, and *Jekyll and Hyde* in particular) between his conscious and his unconscious, or what he calls his "Brownies".[13] Although Stevenson does not attribute the trampling scene specifically to the Brownies (in fact he only attributes three scenes in *Jekyll and Hyde* wholly to them), nevertheless it is difficult to resist the idea that the trampling scene in *Phantastes* had strongly affected him (as the letter to Bob shows), and was lurking more or less unconsciously in his mind, ready to emerge as the central image in the shocking opening sequence of *Jekyll and Hyde*.

The next reference to MacDonald in Stevenson's correspondence comes more than a decade later in a letter to W.E. Henley of April 1883 from Hyères in the French Riviera, where Stevenson and his wife Fanny lived from March 1883 until they moved to Bournemouth in July 1884. Stevenson sent Henley regular critical responses to *The Magazine of Art*, which Henley edited between 1881 and 1886. This so-called "monthly cricket" that Stevenson sent Henley took the form of responses to published issues of the magazine. Stevenson also commented critically on a list of articles, originally written by Henley for his magazine *London*, on a variety of British authors; Henley's (in the event abortive) plan was to turn these into a book entitled *Living Novelists* (*L4* 85 n.4). The list of Stevenson's responses contains such comments as: "Meredith. It has lines. *I* should rewrite it"; "Blackmore. Overhaul. Don't you like the *Maid of Sker*? Madman!" (*L4* 98) When it comes to Henley's piece on MacDonald, Stevenson comments: "MacDonald. Some cuts. Fifteen minutes of touching. Good." (ibid.) He adds with reference to MacDonald's friend Charles Dodgson: "Carroll. Heu! One of the doubtfuls, but some good fooling at the start." (ibid.)

It was also from Hyères in the following year that Stevenson offered his warmest tribute to MacDonald. This comes in a letter of March 1884 from Stevenson to Alfred Dowson, father of Ernest Dowson, the *poète maudit* of the 1890s. Stevenson had got to know the Dowsons eleven years previously when they had all been resident at the Riviera resort of Mentone (or Menton). It was the six-year-old Ernest who had fetched for Stevenson, high on opium, the bunch of violets that occasioned the following ecstasy:

The first violet. There is more secret trouble for the heart in the breath of

---

[13] "A Chapter on Dreams" in *Further Memories* (Tusitala Edition vol. 30) (London: Heinemann, 1924), pp. 41-53.

this small flower, than in all the wines of all the vineyards of Europe. I cannot contain myself. I do not think so small a thing has ever given me such a princely festival of pleasure. I am quite drunken at heart. The first breath, veiled and timid as it seems, maddens and transfigures and transports you out of yourself ... It is like a wind blowing out of fairyland.—No one need tell me that the phrase is exaggerated, if I say that this violet *sings*. (*L1* 401)

The fact that we know that Stevenson had read *Phantastes* makes it difficult to resist seeing in the image of the vocal violet a distant echo of the flower-fairies in chapter 3 of *Phantastes* who "talked singing" (*Ph* 28). At any rate, it was to Alfred Dowson that Stevenson wrote in 1884, inviting him to visit the Stevensons at Hyères, if he were travelling along the Riviera from Mentone. Stevenson then asks Dowson: "Will you also salute Mr MacDonald [at nearby Bordighera] from me? I have had great pleasure from his works." (*L4* 243)

The final reference to MacDonald that I can find in Stevenson's correspondence comes in a letter to W.E. Henley of October 1887 from Saranac Lake, a health resort in the Adirondacks in upper New York State. Stevenson is discussing Gleeson White's 1887 anthology *Ballades and Rondeaus*, at the beginning of which Stevenson and MacDonald stand together, with Stevenson receiving the dedication, and MacDonald providing the epigraph. The fitness of the dedication derives from Stevenson's role as "among the earliest to experiment in these French rhythms, and to introduce Charles d'Orléans and François Villon to the majority of English readers."[14] The epigraph comes from chapter 11 of MacDonald's *Home Again*, published in 1887, and discusses:

these old French ways of verse making that have been coming into fashion of late. Surely they say a pretty thing more prettily for their quaint old-fashioned liberty! That *triolet*—how deliciously impertinent it is! ...Their fantastic surprises, the ring of their bell-like returns on themselves, their music of triangle and cymbal. In some of them poetry seems to approach the nearest possible to bird-song—to unconscious seeming through the most unconscious art, imitating the carelessness and impromptu of forms as old as the existence of birds, and as new as every fresh individual joy in each new generation.

In this letter to Henley, Stevenson gives high praise to the former's work, which is largely represented in the anthology. He opines that, apart from one piece, Andrew Lang "cuts a poor figure" (*L6* 26). Although MacDonald has several triolets in the anthology, it is his rondels that

---

[14] On Stevenson and rondels see William Gray, *Robert Louis Stevenson*, pp. 37-38.

Stevenson singles out for comment: "G. MacDonald comes out strong in his two pious rondels." (*L6* 26) These "Two Rondels" had appeared in *A Threefold Cord* in 1883. One can guess why the following lines might have appealed to Stevenson, the night terrors of whose childhood were expressed in the "North-West Passage" sequence of *A Child's Garden of Verses*, including the famous "Shadow March"; who also compared his bed to a little boat ("My Bed is a Boat"); and who had more than a passing interest in pirates:

> When on the mid sea of the night,
> I waken at thy call, O Lord.
> The first that troop my bark aboard
> Are darksome imps that hate the light,
> Whose tongues are arrows, eyes a blight—
> Of wraths and cares a pirate horde –
> Though on the mid sea of the night
> It was thy call that waked me, Lord.[15]

The resolution of the "Two Rondels" might also have appealed to Stevenson, who like MacDonald had wrestled with Calvinism and its "martinet of a God";[16] this resolution resists any *deus ex machina* and finds instead a kind of inner light which is, so to speak, in tune with the infinite:

> There comes no voice; I hear no word!
> But in my soul dawns something bright:—
> There is no sea, no foe to fight!
> Thy heart and mine beat one accord:
> I need no voice from thee, O Lord,
> Across the mid sea of the night.

Here indeed, as Stevenson puts it, "G. MacDonald comes out strong."

---

[15] See *The Poetical Works of George MacDonald* (2 vols) (London: Chatto & Windus, 1893) vol. II, p, 211, where the rondels appear with slight differences from the version in Gleeson White's anthology.

[16] Unspoken Sermons, 3rd Series 161, Quoted in William Raeper, *George MacDonald* (Tring: Lion, 1987) p. 242.

CHAPTER FOUR

THE INCOMPLETE FAIRY TALES
OF ROBERT LOUIS STEVENSON

The volume entitled *Island Nights' Entertainments* that appeared in 1893 was a far cry from Robert Louis Stevenson's original intentions. The title, with its allusion to *The Arabian Nights*, had originally been intended for "a substantive volume"[1], "a volume of *Märchen* [or fairy tales] which [he] was slowly to elaborate", and of which, as Stevenson wrote to Sidney Colvin in December 1892, "The Bottle Imp" was to have been the "*pièce de résistance*" and "centre piece" (*L7* 436; 461). However, because "The Beach of Falesá" was too short to be published on its own, Colvin had earlier that year taken the unilateral decision to lump it together with "The Bottle Imp" in one volume. By the time Stevenson found out about this initiative in August 1892, it had got as far as being advertised in *The Scotsman*, which incensed Stevenson so much that he would not communicate directly with Colvin about the matter; as he later admitted to Colvin, he had been "much too disappointed to answer", and "annoyed" about the use—actually the misuse—of "The Bottle Imp" (*L7* 436; 461). In the August, Stevenson had asked Charles Baxter to tell Colvin that "The Beach of Falesá" "is *simply not* [Stevenson's emphasis] to appear along with 'The Bottle Imp', [which was] a story of a totally different scope and intention" (*L7* 350). Nevertheless, Colvin had by this time arranged for Cassell to print the two pieces together, in the so-called "Trial Issue". By December, Stevenson had given in to the demands of Colvin and Cassell; he agreed to use the title *Island Nights' Entertainments* for the whole volume which contained both "The Beach of Falesá" and "The Bottle Imp", as well as one or two other stories. However, Stevenson stipulated that "The Beach of Falesá" was to be separated from the other stories by a "fresh false title: ISLAND NIGHTS' ENTERTAINMENTS" (*L7* 436).

---

[1] Bradford A. Booth and Ernest Mehew (eds), *The Letters of Robert Louis Stevenson* (in 8 volumes) (New Haven: Yale UP, 1994-5), vol. 7, p. 350. This edition of RLS's Letters is cited hereafter in parentheses as *L 1-8*.

Stevenson's wishes were not respected even in this matter, for in the edition published by Cassell there is no separation and no false title.

Barry Menikoff has written a book about the myriad cuts and alterations made by the publishers to the manuscript of "The Beach of Falesá."[2] Less attention has been paid to another casualty of the pressures of Victorian publishing, Stevenson's volume of *Märchen*, with which, Stevenson insisted, "The Beach of Falesá" had absolutely nothing to do, being "the child of a quite different inspiration" (*L7* 436). While Stevenson admitted that "that volume [of *Märchen* or fairy tales] might never have got done" (*L7* 436), it is tempting to wonder what such a volume might have looked like if Stevenson had managed to complete it. The lexical choice of "*Märchen*" is itself interesting. "*Märchen*" is a German term that has no exact English equivalent, hovering between the English "fairy tale" and "folk-tale". Stevenson does use the term "folk-tale", for example, calling "The Song of Rahéro" "a perfect folk tale"[3], and in the "Graveyard Stories" chapter of *In the South Seas* referring to a Dr. Sierich "whose collection of folk-tales [Stevenson] expect[ed] with a high degree of interest".[4] Since Stevenson was ready to use the term "folk-tale" when the occasion demanded, it is interesting that in writing to Colvin he chose to use the phrase "a volume of *Märchen*". (*L7* 461) This suggests that "*Märchen*" is being used not in its meaning of "folk-tale", but in its alternative meaning of "fairy tale". As Mary Beth Stein points out in her article on "Folklore and Fairy Tales" in *The Oxford Companion to Fairy Tales*: "In German academic and popular usage *Märchen* refers to the literary fairy tale as well as the traditional folk-tale".[5] Thus *Märchen* can mean *Kunstmärchen* (literary fairy tale) in distinction to *Volksmärchen* (traditional folk-tale), though that distinction does not of course preclude the former from taking up and elaborating elements from the latter. And that, I would suggest, is precisely what Stevenson is doing in his *Märchen* or *literary* fairy tales "The Bottle Imp" and "The Isle of Voices" (and arguably also "The Waif Woman").

Much ink has been spilled in trying to define the relationship between the fairy tale and *fantasy* writing. One of the characteristics of the *literary*

---

[2] Barry Menikoff, *Robert Louis Stevenson and 'The Beach of Falesá': A Study in Victorian Publishing* (Stanford: Stanford University Press, 1984).
[3] Letter of October or November 1891 to H.B. Baildon (*L7 187*).
[4] *In the South Seas* (Tusitala Edition vol.20) (London: Heinemann, 1924), p.173. Sierich's folk-tales were published as "Samoanische Märchen" between 1900-4 in *Internationales Archiv für Ethnographie*.
[5] Jack Zipes (ed.), *The Oxford Companion to Fairy Tales* (Oxford: Oxford University Press, 2000), p.167.

fairy tale, which aligns it with fantasy literature rather than the traditional folk-tale, is the tendency to set the magical elements (often a magical other world) in some tension with the real world. This tension seems to derive particularly from the historical connection between the literary fairy tale and German Romanticism. Thus, at the beginning of George MacDonald's ground-breaking *Phantastes* (1858) (which Stevenson refers to in a letter of 1872[6]), MacDonald places a lengthy quotation from the German arch-Romantic Novalis about the nature of the *Märchen*. *Phantastes* arguably mediated into English literary culture the German Romantic emphasis on magical other worlds which seems to characterise so much British fantasy literature, from MacDonald's friend Lewis Carroll through E. Nesbit to C.S. Lewis and beyond. In this genre the magical elements and the other worlds are played off against *this* world, realistically depicted. Nineteenth century fantasy and fairy tales developed in tension with, and almost as an uncanny double of, nineteenth century Realism. While Stevenson was critical of Realism, and instead promoted Romance as a genre, in his later works written in the South Seas there was a tendency towards an ever grittier realism, for example in *The Ebb-Tide* and also in "The Beach of Falesá", the work Stevenson so determinedly (but in the end vainly) wished to *exclude* from his "volume of *Märchen*". A tendency towards realism is also evident *within* Stevenson's *Märchen*, though this is entirely consistent with a genre that plays off this-worldly trivia against other-worldly charms. Thus Stevenson is insistent that what characterises his *Märchen* is that "[t]hey all have a queer realism, even the most extravagant, even 'The Isle of Voices' : the manners are exact" (*L7* 436).

In Stevenson's *Märchen*, however, what is opposed to the world of magic is not the quotidian world of Dresden, London, or Oxford, but of Hawaii. "The Isle of Voices" does not take place (like the arguably derivative chapter "The Island of the Voices" in C.S. Lewis's *The Voyage of the Dawn Treader*) in some fantasy realm like Narnia; on the contrary, it is set with considerable geographical precision in the South Seas. Although we know from the first paragraph of "The Isle of Voices" that Kalamake, the father-in-law of the hero Keola, is a wizard who would go

---

[6] In a letter to his cousin Bob *(L1* 255), RLS refers to a scene in *Phantastes* where "wooden effigies" of men trample on a little beggar girl (*Phantastes* (London: Dent, 1915), pp. 219-22). The image of a wooden automaton walking over a little girl seems uncannily similar to the beginning of *Strange Case of Dr Jekyll and Mr Hyde* where Hyde "trampled calmly over the child's body and left her screaming on the ground … It wasn't like a man; it was like some damned Juggernaut" (*Ph* 3). See Chapter Three above, "Strange Case of Dr MacDonald and Mr Hyde: Robert Louis Stevenson and George MacDonald.

"into the region of the hobgoblins, and there … lay snares to entrap the spirits of ancient", nevertheless the setting is resolutely nineteenth century *petit bourgeois*, complete with a photograph of Queen Victoria on the parlour wall and a family Bible on the table. Although supposedly on the Hawaian island of Molokai, Kalamake's parlour is actually based on that of ex-judge Hahinu, at whose home in Hookena, on the Kona coast of the island of Hawaii, Stevenson had stayed in April 1889. As Stevenson later wrote: "All that I found in that house, beyond the speech and a few exotic dishes on the table, would have been familiar and exemplary in Europe."[7] There is also a precise geographical location for the mysterious island that Kalamake (along with sorcerers from all ends of the earth) visits on a magic mat to collect shells that mysteriously turn into silver dollars. This island is in the Low or Dangerous Archipelago—the Paumotu Archipelago where Stevenson had heard Donat-Rimarau (who is actually referred to in "The Isle of Voices") narrate many of the "Graveyard Stories" of *In the South Seas*. With a delightful twist of logic, Stevenson has Keola and his wife Lehua consult an atlas to check whether Kalamake, who can make himself swell to gigantic proportions, will be able to cover the distance from the Dangerous Archipelago back to Molokai!

There seems to be no *particular* source for "The Isle of Voices". In her Prefatory Note to *Island Nights' Entertainments* Fanny Stevenson claims that, when writing "The Isle of Voices", her husband had in mind the stories told to the Stevensons by M. Rimareau (sic) in Fakarava in the Paumotu Archipelago. Roslyn Jolly has noted a couple of allusions to motifs from Hawaiian myth and legend, some of which may derive from Stevenson's study of King Kalakaua's notebooks for his *Legends and Myths of Hawaii; The Fables and Folk-Lore of a Strange People*. In fact Stevenson's approach in "The Isle of Voices" seems to be typical of the practice of many writers of fantasy or literary fairy tales (*Kunstmärchen*) according to Maria Nikolajeva in her article on "Fantasy and Fairy Tales" in *The Oxford Companion to Fairy Tales*. Nikolajeva claims that fantasy is eclectic, taking what it needs from a variety of sources, and "focussing on the clash between the magical and the ordinary, on the unexpected consequences of magic when introduced into everyday life."[8]

In the case of "The Bottle Imp" the situation is rather different, however. In her Prefatory Note, Fanny Stevenson explains RLS's somewhat cryptic note that replaced the original sub-title, "A Cue from an

---

[7] *In the South Seas* (Tusitala Edition vol.20) (London: Heinemann, 1924), p.183.
[8] Jack Zipes (ed.), *The Oxford Companion to Fairy Tales* (Oxford: Oxford University Press, 2000), p.151.

Old Melodrama".[9] The melodrama in question was a version of "The Bottle Imp" which Stevenson had come across in the collection of plays belonging their Bournemouth neighbours, the Shelleys. The fact that Stevenson used the term *Märchen* in connection with "The Bottle Imp" suggests that he was aware that the melodrama was "adapted from an old German legend", as Fanny puts it in her Note, even if he was unacquainted with the originals. These earlier versions of "The Bottle Imp" include an 1810 version by Friedrich de la Motte Fouqué as well as a version in Grimms' *Deutsche Sagen* (1816-8). These ultimately derive from the 17th century picaresque novel by von Grimmelshausen, *Trutz Simplex* (1669), set during the Thirty Years War and featuring the adventures of the same Mother Courage who would later appear in the eponymous play by Bertholt Brecht. In chapter 18 of *Trutz Simplex* Courage buys a bottle which she may only sell at a loss, and which contains a familiar spirit that will bring wealth and success; however to die in possession of the magic bottle entails going straight to Hell. Courage takes maximum advantage of the bottle before fobbing it off (in chapter 22) on one of her many lovers. The main elements of Stevenson's *Märchen* are already present in the 17th century German version. The story seems to have a particular fascination for Germans. In the last few years "The Bottle Imp" has gone the way of many fantasies and has become the basis for a card game. Interestingly, although the game was developed in Germany, under the name "*Der Flaschenteufel*", it is Stevenson's version of "The Bottle Imp" which is foregrounded, despite the fact that all the essential ingredients are already present in the German sources.[10]

In Stevenson's "The Bottle Imp" the traditional German tale is relocated into late nineteenth century Hawaii. Indeed the tale explicitly mentions the house of Nahinu, the ex-judge whom Stevenson stayed with

---

[9] Stevenson's Note replacing his original sub-title can be found in *Island Nights' Entertainments* (Tusitala Edition vol.13) (London: Heinemann, 1924), p.78. It refers to the stage version of "The Bottle Imp" made popular in the early 19th century by "the redoubtable O. Smith" – an actor himself now undoubtedly requiring a note.

[10] Another example of the absorption of "The Bottle Imp" by popular culture is its appearance in Terry Brooks's fantasy novel *Wizard at Large* (1988). A substantial passage from "The Bottle Imp" appears as the epigraph to Brooks's novel, which is derivative of the fantasy tradition running from the German Romantics via George MacDonald. Robert Louis Stevenson and "The Bottle Imp" are explicitly referred in the novel (p. 46), but in fact the imp, renamed as a "Darkling", is only another version of the genie in the lamp. The distinctive feature of "The Bottle Imp" tradition going back to Grimmelshausen, that of the need to resell at an ever diminishing price, is not used by Brooks.

at Hookena, which provided the model for Kalamake's parlour in "The Isle of Voices". Circumstantial details from San Francisco to Papeete are presented with such verisimilitude that a "reality effect" is produced, and thus, as Fanny Stevenson pointed out in her Prefatory Note, a sense of uncertainty is induced in the reader's mind.[11] Without going into the intricacies of Todorov's discrimination of the various shadings in the spectrum running from "the marvellous" through "the fantastic" to "the uncanny", it would seem that Rosemary Jackson's reading of Todorov's "fantastic" seems to fit "The Bottle Imp" pretty convincingly; Jackson writes: "Fantastic narratives confound elements of both the marvellous and the mimetic. They assert that what they are telling is real—relying on the conventions of realistic narrative to do so—and then they proceed to break that assumption of realism by introducing what—within those terms—is manifestly unreal."[12]

In her article on "Fantasy and Fairy Tales" already cited, Nikolajeva suggests that "fantasy is closely connected with the notion of modernity".[13] While this would be true of "The Isle of Voices" and especially "The Bottle Imp", it seems less obviously the case in the third candidate for Stevenson's volume of *Märchen*, "The Waif Woman". Although this tale was finally rejected, apparently at the instigation of Fanny, RLS originally saw it as a companion piece to "The Bottle Imp", even sharing the same kind of sub-title: "A Cue from a Saga" (*L7* 436). "The Waif Woman" is based on Stevenson's enthusiasm for the literary work of William Morris. In November 1881 Stevenson wrote to W.E. Henley that Morris's narrative poem *Sigurd the Volsung* was 'a grrrrreat [sic] poem' ((*L3* 253). Ten years later Stevenson drafted a somewhat sycophantic, if "very impudent", letter to Morris, addressing him simply as "Master", and acknowledging his indebtedness to Morris's poetry, especially to *Sigurd*. Stevenson adds that Morris has now "plunged [him] beyond payment" with the *Saga Library*, that is, Morris and Magnússon's translation of the Icelandic Sagas (*L7* 236), though he also criticises Morris for his use of archaic English (*L7* 237).

Stevenson based "The Waif Woman" on Morris and Magnússon's translation of "The Story of the Ere-Dwellers". As a reason for rejecting "The Waif Woman", Fanny raised the spectre of plagiarism—somewhat

---

[11]*Island Nights' Entertainments* (Tusitala Edition vol.13), p.xii.

[12] Rosemary Jackson, *Fantasy: the Literature of Subversion* (London: Methuen, 1981), p.34.

[13] Jack Zipes (ed.), *The Oxford Companion to Fairy Tales* (Oxford: Oxford University Press, 2000), p.151.

rich, coming from Fanny, after the traumatic 'Nixie' affair![14] It was a case, rather, of Stevenson (to use his own phrase) taking a cue from the saga, just as he took a cue from the legend of "The Bottle Imp"; he was in effect re-working the Icelandic folk-material in much the same way as he had re-worked the originally German folk-material. There are significant differences, however. In the case of "The Bottle Imp" the folk-material is transposed to the South Seas, and the names of the protagonists are changed accordingly. But "The Waif Woman" remains firmly set in medieval Iceland, though Stevenson changes the names of all the characters except the central character Thorgunna. Although much of the saga's action is retained, Stevenson nevertheless did make some significant changes, not the least being that Aud, the main protagonist next to Thorgunna, dies at the end of Stevenson's version, whereas in the original saga, Thurid, the character on whom Aud is based, "got better of her sickness so that she was healed" (translation by Morris and Magnússon). This may have been one of changes to the saga that did not, to Fanny's mind, "improve the thing" (*L7* 437 n.8), though perhaps Fanny's judgment was not entirely disinterested. Although Furnas has taken G.S. Hellman to task for suggesting that Fanny had ulterior motives in wishing to suppress "The Waif Woman"[15], there does seem to be something suspicious in her rather pompous and self-righteous protestation of it being 'too cheap an affair to meddle with the best' (*L7* 437 n.8). Fanny may well have been uneasy with Stevenson's very unsympathetic portrayal of Aud, the greedy and manipulative wife. The key moment in the Saga comes when Thurid inveigles her husband into disobeying Thorgunna's instructions to burn her bed-stuff after her death. This crucial piece of *action*, which provokes the post-mortem "walkings and hauntings" which are the real subject matter of the saga, is developed by Stevenson into a substantial *character* sketch, or indeed character

---

[14] Katharine de Mattos, RLS's cousin and dedicatee of *Strange Case of Dr Jekyll and Mr Hyde*, had written a short story for which she was unable to find a publisher. Fanny Stevenson appropriated and reworked Katharine's story, re-titling it "The Nixie" and securing its publication under her name in Scribner's Magazine in the same year the magazine was featuring a monthly article by RLS. On the appearance of "The Nixie", W.E. Henley wrote to RLS: "It's Katharine's; surely it's Katharine's?" Henley's (not unfounded) suggestion of plagiarism provoked a furious response by RLS, which in effect ended his friendship not only with Henley, but also with Katharine and her brother (and RLS's *alter ego*), Bob Stevenson. For further details of this episode, see William Gray, *Robert Louis Stevenson: A Literary Life* (Palgrave Macmillan, 2004), pp. 104-6.

[15] J.C. Furnas, *Voyage to Windward* (London: Faber & Faber, 1952), p.404.

assassination—literally as well as figuratively, since unlike Thurid, Aud dies. Stevenson's elaboration of motivation and character adds a modern note of realism to the saga, although of the Sagas themselves, RLS wrote to Burlinghame: "talk about realism!" (*L7* 296)

The question whether the exclusion of "The Waif Woman" from *Island Nights' Entertainments* was artistically right was perhaps settled in advance by Colvin's unilateral decision (so bitterly resented by Stevenson) to publish "The Bottle Imp" alongside "The Beach of Falesá". Stevenson wrote to Colvin that "The Waif Woman" and "The Isle of Voices", though not up to the rank of "The Bottle Imp", "each have a certain merit, and they fit in style". (*L7* 436) But "The Waif Woman" would probably have stood out in *Island Nights' Entertainments* as published, since it is not set in the South Seas. However, it could well have fitted into the "volume of *Märchen*" that Stevenson had intended, but for the interference of Colvin, "slowly to elaborate". What else may have found its way into such a volume is a matter of speculation. Apart from whatever new stories Stevenson might have come up with, there is also the question of other material whose final destination was still undecided in 1892. Other *märchenhaft* pieces that might have been candidates for inclusion would surely include some of the tales collected under the rather elastic title *Fables*, and published posthumously in 1896 as an appendix to *Strange Case of Dr Jekyll and Mr Hyde*. Of the history of these *Fables* very little is known, other than that Stevenson first mentions them in the summer of 1874 and was still working on them twenty years later. According to Balfour, Stevenson worked on the *Fables* in 1887, and approached Longmans about their publication in 1888, though he does not seem to have come back to them till near the end of his life. We do not know with any certainty the order in which they were written over that twenty-year period. According to Colvin's guess, some of the earliest written include "those in the vein of Celtic mystery, *The Touchstone, The Poor Thing, The Song of the Morrow*".[16] Balfour, however, writing of the years 1891-94, suggests that:

> [T]he reference to Odin [in *Fable* 16] perhaps is due to [Stevenson's] reading of the Sagas, which led him to attempt a tale in the same style, called "The Waif Woman". But I could find no clue to any fresh study of the Celtic legends, that would have suggested the last and most beautiful

---

[16] *The Letters of Robert Louis Stevenson* (Vol. 1) (ed Colvin) (Tusitala Edition vol.31) (London: Heinemann, 1924), p. 174.

fable of all, called "The Song of the Morrow". [17]

Balfour seems to be suggesting that "The Song of the Morrow" came out of roughly the same context as "The Waif Woman". Had Colvin's precipitate action not in a sense forced Stevenson's hand, and narrowed his options in terms of a "volume of *Märchen*", then some of those stories "running to a greater length, and conceived in a more mystic and legendary vein" (as Colvin puts it in his Prefatory Note to the *Fables* [18]) might perhaps have found their way into Stevenson's sadly incomplete book of fairy tales.

---

[17] Graham Balfour, *The Life of Robert Louis Stevenson* [1901] (One Volume Edition) (London: Methuen, 1906), p. 360.

[18] *The Strange Case of Dr Jekyll and Mr Hyde; Fables* (Tusitala Edition vol.5) (London: Heinemann, 1924), p. 77.

CHAPTER FIVE

DEATH, MYTH AND REALITY IN C.S. LEWIS

C.S. Lewis's imaginative writing is all about death. It is about the impact on a nine-year-old-boy of the death of his mother. Lewis's writing itself could be seen as an attempt to come to terms with that death by the very act of writing. The author's life and work cannot be neatly separated, despite the fact that in an early critical work, *The Personal Heresy,* Lewis tried to direct critical attention away from the author and towards the text.[1] However, I suspect we would have been able to guess the secret theme of Lewis's writing (the figure in his carpet) even if he had not given the game away in his autobiography *Surprised by Joy: the shape of my early life.* There Lewis rather laconically tells us of his mother's death when he was nine. Only a few phrases give away the impact this event had on his life. The section ends in lapidary fashion:

> With my mother's death all settled happiness, all that was tranquil and reliable, disappeared from my life. There was to be much fun, many pleasures, many stabs of Joy; but no more of the old security. It was sea and islands now; the great continent had sunk like Atlantis.[2]

More revealing perhaps of the personal anguish of the nine-year old boy is: "There came a night when I was ill and crying both with headache and toothache and distressed because my mother did not come to me." (*SBJ* 20) In these circumstances the natural resort would be to the father, but at this point Lewis effectively lost his father too, though this loss to Lewis is

---

[1] In C.S. Lewis and E.M.W. Tillyard, *The Personal Heresy: A Controversy* (London, Oxford University Press, 1939), Lewis denied that the reading of literature is in the first place a matter of *"knowing* or *getting into touch with"* a writer (p. 9; Lewis's emphasis). Rather, he maintained, "when we read poetry as poetry should be read, we have before us no representation which claims to be the poet, and frequently no representation of a *man,* a *character,* or a *personality* at all" (p. 4; Lewis's emphasis).

[2] *Surprised by Joy: The shape of my early life* [1955] (London: Collins Fontana, 1959), p. 23. Hereafter cited in parentheses as *SBJ*.

defensively disguised as a loss to the father:

> His nerves had never been of the steadiest and his emotions had always been uncontrolled. Under the pressure of anxiety his temper became incalculable; he spoke wildly and acted unjustly. Thus by a peculiar cruelty of fate, during those months the unfortunate man, had he but known it, was really losing his sons as well as his wife. (*SBJ* 21)

One result of these losses was a very close bond between Lewis and his brother which lasted all his life (Lewis died in his brother's arms). There was also the development of an intense imaginative life, and the creation of an imaginary other world: "Animal-Land". Lewis denied that "Animal-Land" had much in common with Narnia because it lacked a sense of imaginative wonder (*SBJ* 18), but Lewis's experiences of imaginative wonder—or Joy—were also beginning at this time. Narnia, it could be argued, pulls together different kinds of imaginative experience which were split apart in the young Lewis.

What *The Chronicles of Narnia* offered was an imaginary realm where Lewis tried retrospectively to work through his sense of cataclysmic loss, and to quest after what his heart ached for, the sense of the "enormous bliss" of Eden—Milton's phrase, characteristically borrowed by Lewis (*SBJ* 19). The word Lewis uses most often for this lost bliss is "Joy"—the title *Surprised by Joy* is again borrowed, this time from Wordsworth. Where Lewis found Joy evoked above all was in "myth". But myth for Lewis, up until his conversion in 1931, was by definition "not true". Myths were "breathing a lie through Silver", to use Lewis's phrase quoted by Tolkien in his introduction to his poem "Mythopoeia"—a poem occasioned by a great debate between Lewis and Tolkien just before Lewis's conversion.[3] One result of his conversion was that Lewis no longer thought that myths were "lies", but "true" insofar as they pointed to the central myth of Christ which was "in fact" true. Here was a myth of a dying and rising God that had really happened (*SBJ* 187-189). Other myths could have some measure of "truth" insofar as they referred unconsciously to the "true" myth of Christ. This is the old Christian idea of the Greek poets being—like the Hebrew prophets—a *preparatio evangelica* [preparation for the gospel]. Lewis was close to Bede Griffiths (to whom *Surprised by Joy* was dedicated) and was open to the "truth" of Hindu

---

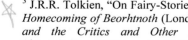

[3] J.R.R. Tolkien, "On Fairy-Stories", *Tree and Leaf; Smith of Wootton Major; The Homecoming of Beorhtnoth* (London: Unwin, 1975), p. 55; see also *The Monsters and the Critics and Other Essays* (ed Christopher Tolkien) (London: HarperCollins, 2006), pp. 145ff. Hereafter cited in parentheses *MCOE*.

myths[4]. Indeed, just as T.S. Eliot had earlier hesitated between Christianity and Buddhism, Lewis says that for him it was a choice of whether to convert to Christianity or to Hinduism (*SBJ* 188). Lewis was certainly not a religious pluralist; but on the other hand he was not, like the conservative evangelicals who have appropriated him, an exclusivist. In his religious inclusivism he actually seems quite close to the spirit of Vatican II.

But the confidence with which Lewis asserted the truth "in fact" of Christianity, a confidence which informs his popular apologetics of the 1940s, seems to have evaporated after an apparently (for Lewis) disturbing encounter with the philosopher Elizabeth Anscombe in 1948.[5] In a debate in the Socratic Club in Oxford focusing on Chapter 3 of Lewis's recently published book *Miracles*, it seems that Lewis's *intellectual* argument against philosophical scepticism was soundly refuted by Anscombe, a pupil of Wittgenstein, and also, incidentally, a Roman Catholic. It was not Lewis's *faith,* then, which was under attack, but his *reasoning.* Whether as a result of this encounter or not, the flow of confident rational defences by Lewis of the truth "in fact" of Christianity ceased, and he turned instead to *The Chronicles of Narnia.* It is as if he recognized that rational argument was not the best way to communicate the truth of Christianity (or at least that he was no longer the best person to do this); *myth* began to seem a better way to communicate the truth of Christianity. Lewis, who in a professional sense knew what he was talking about, denied that *The Chronicles of Narnia* were *allegory.* By this he meant that the stories were not personifications of Christian doctrine. Rather, certain pictures seem to have come to him as "dream-images". As he put it in "It All Began with a Picture":

> All my seven Narnian books, and my three science fiction books, began with seeing pictures in my head. At first they were not a story, just pictures. The *Lion* all began with a picture of a Faun carrying an umbrella and parcels in a snowy wood. This picture had been in my mind since I was about sixteen. When I was about forty, I said to myself: "Let's try to

---

[4] A former student of Lewis, Bede Griffiths was a Benedictine monk who moved to India, finally settling at the ashram of Shantivanam. While remaining a Catholic monk, he adopted the trappings of Hindu monastic life and entered into dialogue with Hindu thought, studying with Raimundo Panikkar (author of *The Unknown Christ Of Hinduism* (1981)), and writing many books on Hindu-Christian dialogue, including *Christ in India: Essays Towards a Hindu-Christian Dialogue* (1967) and *Return to the Centre*, (1976). See his autobiography *The Golden String* (1954).

[5] For further references to Lewis's encounter with Anscombe see Chapter Seven below,"The Lion, the Witch and the Atlantean Box: Psychoanalysis and Narnia Revisited", note 1.

make a story about it." At first I had very little idea how the story would go. But then suddenly Aslan came bounding into it. I think I had been having a good many dreams about lions about this time.[6]

What Lewis is returning to in *The Chronicles of Narnia* is the power of "pictures". In *The Pilgrim's Regress* he explicitly calls the "pagan" myths "pictures", and affirms them as a *preparatio evangelica* [preparation for the gospel].[7] They are God's way of communicating himself apart from Christ, who is the reality to whom the pictures point. It is as if in *The Chronicles of Narnia* (as in his science fiction works) Lewis is creating a new world where he can imagine "pictures", or "myths" which would express in *that* world what the "true" myth of Christ means in our world. To play with Lewis's own phrase, Lewis is now "breathing the *truth* through Silver", and Aslan is "the unknown Christ of Narnia".

We may suspect, however, that Lewis's longing for another country which he identifies in the epigraph to the last chapter of *Surprised by Joy* as Augustine's "land of peace", is actually a longing for the lost Atlantis, that is, for the settled, *reliable* happiness which went with his mother, and originally with his mother's body. Then the creation of another world where Joy is offered in the body (and especially in *the mane)* of Aslan takes on another resonance. Lewis would thus be returning to the realm of "the semiotic" (in Kristeva's terminology) to seek the lost wholeness which went with the feel and the touch of the mother's body, and the look of her face. One of the most powerful evocations of what Lewis was looking for in Narnia comes in the last chapter of *The Magician's Nephew,* where he writes:

> Both the children were looking up into the Lion's face as he spoke these words. And all at once (they never knew exactly how it happened) the face seemed to be a sea of tossing gold in which they were floating, and such a sweetness and power rolled about them and over them and entered them that they felt they had never really been happy or wise or good, or even alive and awake, before. And the memory of that moment stayed with them always, so that as long as they both lived, if ever they were sad or afraid or angry, the thought of all that golden goodness, and the feeling that it was still there, quite close, just round some corner or just behind some door, would come back and make them sure, deep down inside, that

---

[6] C.S. Lewis, *Of This and Other Worlds* (London: Collins, 1982**)**, p. 79.
[7] C.S. Lewis, *The Pilgrim's Regress* [1933] (Glasgow: Collins Fount, 1977), pp. 192-202; see also C.S. Lewis, *Selected Books* (London: HarperCollins, 2002), pp. 167-75.

all was well.[8]

The fact that Aslan is male does not necessarily tell against the reading of such passages as representations of the "primary maternal matrix". Certainly David Holbrook in his psychoanalytical reading of *The Chronicles of Narnia* in his book *The Skeleton in the Wardrobe* presents Aslan as "the Good Mother (or Breast)"[9]—with the Witch figuring as the split-off "Bad Mother (or Breast)".[10] In any case we seem here to be in the realm of "the imaginary" or "the semiotic"[11]—the pre-oedipal realm where in psychoanalytical terms "objects" (or, in less technical language, individual "subjects"[12]) have not yet been constituted, let alone gendered. Indeed, somewhat controversially, Kristeva does actually posit a role for the ("imaginary") father in this pre-oedipal scenario.[13] The dying mother of Digory, who of all the Narnian characters is closest to Lewis himself and who will grow up to be the Professor in *The Lion, the Witch and the Wardrobe,* appears in the final chapter of *The Magician's Nephew* when Digory brings her what *he* has gone to Narnia to find, the Apple of Youth. *The Magician's Nephew* is haunted by the figure of Digory's dying mother, to whom we are introduced in the first chapter. The way into Narnia is provided by magic rings made from dust in an ancient box surviving from—significantly—Atlantis. At the end of *The Magician's Nephew*, Digory's mother eats the Apple of Youth and recovers. Thus Lewis brings about in the magic of fiction what his prayers as a nine-year-old boy could not achieve—the restoration to life of his dying mother. The core of the magic apple is planted and grows into a Narnian tree flourishing in the London suburbs, and will eventually provide the timber for the eponymous wardrobe.

However, this fictional or imaginary restoration to life of the dying

---

[8] C.S. Lewis, *The Magician's Nephew* [1955] (London: Harper Collins, 1996), p. 165. Hereafter cited in parentheses as *MN*.
[9] David Holbrook, *The Skeleton in the Wardrobe: C.S. Lewis' Fantasies: A Phenomenological Study* (Lewisburg: Bucknell University Press, 1991), p. 162.
[10] Ibid., p. 41.
[11] On the "semiotic" and the "*chora*" see Julia Kristeva, *Revolution in Poetic Language* (trans. Margaret Waller) (New York: Columbia University Press, 1984); extracts in *The Kristeva Reader* (ed Toril Moi) (Oxford: Blackwell, 1986).
[12] In "object relations theory", "objects" include, but are not restricted to, human subjects (there are for example "transitional objects" such as Linus's famous blanket in *Peanuts*).
[13] Julia Kristeva, *Tales of Love* (New York: Columbia University Press, 1987), p.46. See also Chapter One above where I refer to Kristeva's discussion in *Black Sun* of the pre-oedipal "father in individual prehistory".

mother is not without its complications. If it were a straightforward reversal of what happened in real life, it would merely be escapist fantasy, sheer wish-fulfilment. As Lewis tells us in *Surprised by Joy,* his prayers for a miracle were not answered (*SBJ* 22). Somehow his fiction must achieve an imaginary transformation of reality without becoming a gross distortion of reality. The "picture" Lewis is offering in *The Magician's Nephew* must be a myth but not a lie. Lewis seeks to achieve this compromise by giving a version of the Genesis temptation story in which the Fall does not occur. *The Magician's Nephew* can be seen as the Narnian Genesis. Digory's temptation in relation to the Apple of Youth, also called the Apple of Life, clearly echoes the Biblical narrative. There is a precedent in Lewis's science-fiction novel *Perelandra* for a version of the Genesis temptation story in which the Fall is avoided. In *The Magician's Nephew* Digory is set the task of bringing to Aslan an apple from the garden beyond the western borders of Narnia. When he reaches the garden and picks the apple, he finds the witch Jadis waiting for him. Digory had woken Jadis unwittingly (if culpably, since he ignored warnings against ringing a magic bell) from an enchanted sleep in the dead world of Charn; and he had unwillingly brought her to Narnia, where she will appear many years later as the White Witch of *The Lion, the Witch and the Wardrobe.* Jadis is also related to the Green Witch in *The Silver Chair* who takes the form of a serpent[14]. Jadis tempts Digory to eat the apple himself, or, in a much more terrible temptation, to take it back to his dying mother, rather than bringing it to Aslan. This is like a re-enactment of Lewis's own childhood trauma: obedience to God's will seems to mean acceptance of his mother's death. Digory manages to resist this overwhelming temptation to disobedience, and returns to Aslan with the apple. Had Digory been disobedient, Aslan tells him, the apple would have healed his mother, "but not to your joy or hers. The day would have come when both you and she would have looked back and said it would have been better to die in that illness." (*MN* 163) Digory seems resigned to the bitter truth of this:

> Digory could say nothing, for tears choked him and he gave up hopes of saving his Mother's life, but at the same time he knew that the Lion knew what would have happened, and that there might be things more terrible even than losing someone you love by death. (*MN* 163)

---

[14] There has been some speculation that the Green Witch *is* Jadis, but there is no textual evidence for this. See, for example, Elizabeth Baird Hardy, *Milton, Spenser and the Chronicles of Narnia: Literary Sources for the C.S. Lewis Novels* (Jefferson, N.C.: McFarland, 2007), pp. 38-9.

Then, in an example of the "joyous turn" or "*eucatastrophe*" which, according to Tolkien's "On Fairy-Stories", characterizes the fairy-tale and brings consolation to the reader (*MCOE* 153), "it was as if the whole world had turned inside out and upside down" (*MN 163*). Aslan tells Digory to pluck another apple for his mother, and subsequently she is miraculously cured. Whether this is a myth "breathing the truth through Silver", or a lie which denies the horror of reality; whether it represents a pathetic attempt by the middle-aged Lewis to console himself with fantasy for the blighting of his emotional life by the death of his mother, or is a creative attempt to transpose the truth of the Christian myth into a personal mythology: these questions must presumably be left to the judgment of the individual reader. That decision will, however, be related to the way we read other significant actions in *The Chronicles of Narnia:* these would have to include the Passion and Resurrection narratives (of Aslan) in *The Lion, the Witch and the Wardrobe* and the Narnian Apocalypse in *The Last Battle.* There is hardly room here to consider either of these in any detail. In each case, however, the crucial question would be: how real does death feel in these narratives? There are some problems with the Narnian Passion narratives, but overall the death of Aslan does carry weight, though mostly this is derived from the power of the very transparently underlying Christian myth. The ending of *The Last Battle* falls into two parts: first there is the Narnian Apocalypse, which works rather effectively as a pastiche of the Biblical book of Revelation; secondly there is the more problematic life-after-death sequence which is explicitly based on Platonism. As the Professor says: "It's all in Plato, all in Plato: bless me, what *do* they teach them at these schools!"[15] All the sons of Adam and daughters of Eve (apart from the lapsed Susan[16]) who have been to Narnia are reunited in the Platonic "real Narnia". It transpires that they have all been killed in a railway accident, though admittedly the tone in which this is narrated can seem disconcertingly light. Edmund says:

> There was a frightful roar and something hit me with a bang, but it didn't hurt. And I felt not so much scared as—well, excited. Oh—and this one queer thing. I'd a rather sore knee, from a hack at rugger. I noticed it had suddenly gone. And I felt very light. And then—here we were. (*LB* 130-1)

This could hardly be said to treat death with real existential seriousness,

---

[15] C.S. Lewis, *The Last Battle* [1956] (London, Harper Collins, 1996), p. 160. Hereafter cited in parentheses as *LB*

[16] The controversial case of Susan Pevensie is discussed in Chapter Eight below, "Pullman, Lewis, MacDonald and the anxiety of influence".

which of course undermines the story's ability to offer any real resolution to the problem—or mystery—of death.

Where death *is* treated with a profoundly existential seriousness is in Lewis's account of his own bereavement. At first not intended for publication, and subsequently published under a pseudonym, *A Grief Observed* was only published under Lewis's own name after his death. In the last decade of his life Lewis had experienced, he said, the happiness that had passed him by in his twenties. He fell in love with and married (or perhaps vice versa) Joy Davidman Gresham. Joy was already dying when Lewis fell in love with her; indeed she was a dying mother of two boys. Lewis himself commented on the uncanny similarities between the circumstances of his own mother's death and those of Joy's. It is almost as if, having failed to come to terms with his mother's death in the early part of his life, or subsequently through the medium of imaginative fiction, Lewis had to work through that death again by repeating the experience of it in later life. The story of this loss, that is, the loss of Joy that repeated the loss of his mother, is narrated in the most harrowingly realistic terms. *A Grief Observed* is about the smashing of all images, of all "pictures", by the reality of death. If there had been the suggestion of consoling fantasy in the Narnia books, it is rudely dismissed now:

> [D]on't come to me talking about the consolations of religion or I shall suspect that you don't understand. Unless, of course, you can literally believe all that stuff about family reunions "on the further shore", pictured in entirely earthly terms. But that is all unscriptural, all out of bad hymns and lithographs. There's not a word of it in the Bible. And it rings false. We *know* it couldn't be like that.[17]

A couple of pages later he adds: "Come, what do we gain by evasions? We are under the harrow and can't escape. Reality, looked at steadily, is unbearable." (*AGO* 25)

Reality is iconoclastic (*AGO* 52), shattering all the ideas we have spun to protect and console ourselves. Real life, and especially real death, is precisely not a novel, not a fiction—and this is coming from a man quite conscious of the fact that from his youth his life had always already been structured by his reading of literature. But in reality, he has learned that "you never know how much you really believe anything until its truth or falsehood becomes a matter of life and death to you." (*AGO* 21) In the end Lewis found all his dreams and his faith smashed by the reality of death.

---

[17] C.S. Lewis, *A Grief Observed* [published under the pseudonym N.W. Clerk 1961; reprinted under Lewis's name in 1964] (London: Faber, 1966), p.23. Hereafter cited in parentheses as *AGO*.

Reality, looked at steadily, is unbearable.

Yet Lewis survived, and survived by writing, by writing *this* book. It was, he says, "a defence against total collapse" (*AGO* 47). And at the very end, incorrigibly, almost defiantly, Lewis finishes this narrative about the uselessness of stories in face of the reality of death—with a quotation from one of the most perfect and serene pieces of literature ever written in praise of life and light and love, Dante's *Paradiso.* Of course the quotation is about the smile of a grace-filled woman whom the poet has lost, and hopes to find again after death. In *Canto XXXI* Dante sees Beatrice "in all her glory crowned/by the reflections of eternal light" (11. 71-72) and addresses to her the following prayer (it is with the last line of this extract— "*poi si tornò all'eterna fontana*"—that Lewis concludes *A Grief Observed*):

> "O lady in whom all my hope takes strength,
> and who for my salvation did endure
> to leave her footprints on the floor of Hell,
> through your own power, through your own excellence
> I recognize the grace and the effect
> of all those things I have seen with my eyes.
>
> From bondage into freedom you led me
> by all those paths, by using all those means
> which were within the limits of your power.
> Preserve in me your great munificence,
> so that my soul which you have healed may be
> pleasing to you when it slips from the flesh."
>
> Such was my prayer. And she, so far away,
> or so it seemed, looked down at me and smiled;
> then to Eternal Light she turned once more.[18]

---

[18] *Paradiso*, Canto XXXI, 11. 79—93; translation from Mark Musa, (ed.) (1995) *The Portable Dante* (New York: Penguin, 1995), pp. 571-2.

CHAPTER SIX

SPIRITUALITY AND THE PLEASURE
OF THE TEXT: C.S. LEWIS AND THE ACT
OF READING

The character in C. S. Lewis's fiction who is most concerned about spirituality is Edward Weston, the mad, bad scientist of *Out of the Silent Planet* and *Perelandra*. Weston's interest in spirituality emerges in a bizarre episode on the planet Perelandra (or Venus), when Weston engages Ransom, the hero of Lewis's science fiction trilogy, in a philosophical argument more suited to "a Cambridge combination [common] room" than to such "conditions of inconceivable strangeness".[1] In this exchange Weston informs Ransom that, during his convalescence after the exertions of his expedition to Malacandra (or Mars) described in *Out of the Silent Planet*, he has developed a keen interest in spirituality. This new stage in Weston's personal development has taken him beyond what Lewis calls (though not in the trilogy itself) "Westonism": that is, the quasi-religious faith that humankind can achieve some kind of immortality by constantly colonizing other planets. After the voyage to Malacandra, however, this dream of interplanetary colonization has in principle been realized, and Weston now feels led beyond "mere Westonism". He has become disillusioned with the traditional dualism of "Man" and "Nature", and thinks that this binary opposition (as we might call it nowadays) breaks down when we contemplate "the unfolding of the cosmic process" (*CT* 224). He is now "a convinced believer in emergent evolution" (ibid.), that is, in a mishmash of Bergson and other Life-philosophies. For him "the forward movements of Life—growing spirituality—is everything" (*CT* 225). Weston's mission henceforth is no longer merely to spread the human race (via interplanetary travel), but "to spread spirituality" (ibid.).

---

[1] C.S. Lewis, *The Cosmic Trilogy* (*Out of the Silent Planet* [1938]; *Perelandra* [1943]; *That Hideous Strength* [1945]) (London: Pan Books in association with The Bodley Head, 1989), p.223. Hereafter cited in parentheses as *CT*.

The spirituality to which Weston has now dedicated his life has led him to penetrate the crust of "outworn theological technicalities" which surrounds organised religion (ibid.). The underlying "Meaning" and the "essential truth of the religious view of life" is "pure Spirit", "a great, inscrutable Force" that has chosen Weston as its instrument (ibid.). At this point the Lewis persona of the bluff defender of "mere Christianity" appears in the figure of Ransom, who replies, "wrinkling his brow": "I don't know much about what people call the religious view of life ... You see, I'm a Christian." (*CT* 225) He continues, as a chap would: "Look here, one wants to be careful about this sort of thing. There are spirits and spirits, you know ... There's nothing especially fine about simply being a spirit.   The Devil is a spirit." (*CT* 227) But from the perspective of Weston's vitalism, which might be seen as anticipating some of what passes for (post)modern spirituality in at least some Cambridge combination rooms, such binary opposites as God and the Devil, or heaven and hell, are "pure mythology", "doublets [which] are really portraits of Spirit, of cosmic energy". (ibid.) "Your heaven", Weston continues, "is a picture of the perfect spirituality ahead; your hell a picture of the urge or *nisu*s which is driving us on to it from behind." (ibid.) Ransom's obtuseness and timidity in clinging to "the old accursed dualism", "the miserable framework of your old jargon about self and self-sacrifice", leads Weston into a paroxysm of indignation in which he cries: "I *am* the Universe. I, Weston, am your God and your Devil. I call that Force into me completely..." (*CT* 230) There follows an object lesson illustrating Ransom's earlier remark that not all spirits are good for you. It begins when "a spasm like that preceding a deadly vomit twisted Weston's face out of recognition" (ibid.). In a melodramatic transformation scene reminiscent of film versions of *Dr Jekyll and Mr Hyde,* Weston is turned into the hideous "Un-man", the Devil Incarnate of Perelandra.

The link between spirituality and the Devil is also evident in *The Screwtape Letters*, published the year before *Perelandra.* In one of this series of letters from a senior to a junior devil, Screwtape says that "Our Father Below" has never forgiven "the Enemy" for producing creatures which are not, like devils, pure spirit, but a "revolting hybrid", "half-spirit and half-animal".[2] It was this adulteration of spirit that originally caused "Our Father" to "withdraw his support" from "the Enemy"—a withdrawal whose rapidity gave rise to the ridiculous story of some kind of ejection or Fall from Heaven (*SL* 98). "The Enemy" has in Screwtape's view

---

[2] C.S. Lewis, *The Screwtape Letters* [1942] (London: Collins Fontana, 1955), p.44. Hereafter cited in parentheses as *SL.*

degraded "the whole spiritual world by unnatural liaisons with the two-legged animals" (*SL* 17). But the humans do possess an element of spirituality which it will take a long time to remove; in the meantime the tactic is to *corrupt* it (*SL* 116; emphasis in original). Spirituality, or rather, false spirituality, is always to be encouraged, says Screwtape; it disarms prayer by deflecting attention from the body, for whose needs "the Enemy", in his "commonplace, uninteresting way", has commanded the "little vermin" to pray (*SL* 137).

Spirituality is also an indispensable defence against one of the most potent weapons in "the Enemy's" arsenal—pleasure. As Screwtape reminds Wormwood, "the Enemy" is "a hedonist at heart" (*SL* 112; 127). Beneath the façade of "fasts and vigils and stakes and crosses", "the Enemy" offers "pleasure, and more pleasure … pleasures for evermore" (*SL* 112). At all costs Wormwood's "patient" must protected from "*real* pleasure", as opposed to the "vanity, bustle ... and expensive tedium" which Wormwood can palm off on him as pleasure (*SL* 67; emphasis in original). *Real* pleasure, which is a true and disinterested enjoyment of something for its own sake, and not for the sake of convention or fashion, can produce in the humans "a sort of innocence and humility and self-forgetfulness" (*SL* 69). Such humility and self-forgetfulness is a step on the road to the kind of loss of self which "the Enemy" sees as the humans' highest good. The first blunder for which Screwtape chastises Wormwood was to have allowed his patient one of the most dangerous of pleasures: "to read a book he really enjoyed, because he enjoyed it and not in order to make clever remarks about it to his new friends." (*SL* 66-67) Wormwood's second blunder was to have allowed his patient the pleasure of a walk through country he really likes; but it is significant that priority is given to "the pleasure of the text". For Lewis, as we shall see, a human being is practically constituted by the act of reading. While any genuine pleasure would in principle suffice to set a human being on the road to self-transcendence, for Lewis it is above all the pleasure of the text that can lead to the saving "annihilation of the self", as he will later put it in *An Experiment in Criticism*.

The primacy that Lewis gives to the act of reading, the sense that his fundamental way of being is always already "intertextual", can be seen even in his teenage years. At the age of sixteen he wrote to his friend Arthur Greeves:

> You ask whether I have ever been in love: fool as I am, I am not quite such a fool as that. But if one is only to talk from first hand experience on any subject, conversation would be a very poor business. But though I have no personal experience of the thing they call love, I have what is better—the

experience of Sappho, of Euripides, of Catullus, of Shakespeare, of
Spenser, of Austen, of Bronte, of, of, —anyone else I have read. We see
through their eyes.[3]

The idea that in reading literature "we see through their [the writers']
eyes" re-emerges twenty years later in Lewis's essay "The Personal
Heresy". In this attack on what Wimsatt and Beardsley would
subsequently call "the Intentional Fallacy", Lewis declares that we should
look with the poet's eyes, and not *at* him. In order "to see things as the
poet sees them I must share his consciousness and not attend to it",
whatever philosophical difficulties this may entail.[4] Lewis's resistance to
any undue attention to the author and his "personality" derives from his
conviction that the act of reading offers an escape from "personality".
Although he does not acknowledge his closeness to T.S. Eliot on this
point, Lewis does in fact share Eliot's suspicion of "personality", as well
as the latter's deep fear of solipsism (a suspicion and a fear that may
reflect the Idealist philosophical background that Lewis and Eliot had in
common). Literature can enable "a voyage beyond the limits of his [the
reader's as well as the writer's] personal point of view, an annihilation of
the brute fact of his own particular psychology rather than its assertion".[5]
Although "admittedly we can never quite get out of our own skins", as
Lewis was to put it twenty-five years later in *An Experiment in Criticism*,
the reading of literature does seem to offer "a way out". At the very least it
can enable one to "eliminate the grosser illusions of perspective ... If I
can't get out of the dungeon I shall at least look out through the bars. It is
better than sinking back on the straw in the darkest corner."[6]

   If Lewis in *The Personal Heresy* anticipates critics who, from Wimsatt
and Beardsley to Roland Barthes, have proclaimed the demise of the
author, in *An Experiment in Criticism* Lewis heralds the return of the
reader in a way that again seems, *mutatis mutandis*, to anticipate Barthes.
The experiment he proposes is to fix critical attention on "the act of
reading" (*EIC* 104). Books on the shelf are merely "potential literature",
since literature only exists *in actu*, in the "transient experience" of good
readers reading (ibid.). Lewis seems close to those "reader-response"

---

[3] C.S. Lewis, *They Stand Together: The Letters of C. S. Lewis to Arthur Greeves
1914-1963* (ed. Walter Hooper) (London: Collins, 1979), p. 85.
[4] C.S. Lewis and E.M.W. Tillyard, *The Personal Heresy: A Controversy* (London:
Oxford University Press, 1939), pp. 11-12.
[5] Lewis and Tillyard, *The Personal Heresy*, pp. 26-7.
[6] C.S. Lewis, *An Experiment in Criticism* (Cambridge: Cambridge University
Press, 1961), pp. 101-2. Hereafter cited in parentheses as *EIC*.

critics (such as Louise Rosenblatt and Wolfgang Iser) who have emphasized the primacy of the text in an interactive reader-text relationship. There is an element of self-surrender in good reading, which Lewis calls "receiving" the work (*EIC* 19). The opposite of "receiving" a work of art is "using" it. More "subjective" reader-response critics such as David Bleich and the later Norman Holland could be seen in Lewis's terms as "using" rather than "receiving" works of literature. Lewis has an almost sacramental understanding of good reading. Of serious readers he writes:

> [T]he first reading of some literary work is often ... an experience so momentous that only experiences of love, religion or bereavement can furnish a standard of comparison. Their whole consciousness is changed. They have become what they were not before. (*EIC* 3)

Such literary readers live, one might say, "intertextually": "Scenes and characters from books provide them with a sort of iconography by which they interpret or sum up their own experience." (ibid.)

Whatever reservations we may have about Lewis's perhaps over-confident conviction that it is possible to draw a clear line between the life-enhancing "reception" of good literature by the few, and the self-gratifying "use" of bad literature by the many, at least he is not seeking to impose some monolithic canon after the fashion of F.R.Leavis[7]. Although Leavis is not mentioned by name, *An Experiment in Criticism* is among other things a sustained attack on the Leavis school on its own Cambridge turf. It is easy perhaps to underestimate the boldness of Lewis in attacking what he calls "the Vigilant school" in 1961, when Leavis and his followers were still dominant in Cambridge. Whether or not the "literary Puritans" mentioned by Lewis early in *An Experiment in Criticism* are entirely to be identified with the "evaluative" or "Vigilant" critics discussed later, the former certainly have the potential to become the latter. The "literary Puritans" are in their way deeply "spiritual". For them, "the Puritan conscience works on without the Puritan theology—like millstones grinding nothing." (*EIC* 10) The literary Puritan "applies to literature all the scruples, the rigorism, the self-examination, the distrust of pleasure, which his forebears applied to the spiritual life; and perhaps soon all the intolerance and self-righteousness." (ibid.) Such a literary temperament

---

[7] F. R. Leavis (1895-1978) was editor of the periodical *Scrutiny* (1932-53) and the author of several highly influential books including *The Great Tradition* (1948) and *The Common Pursuit* (1952). He emphasized the moral seriousness of literature.

would find itself particularly drawn to the high spiritual calling of the "Vigilant" school, which Lewis describes as follows:

> They are entirely honest, and wholly in earnest. They believe they are smelling out and checking a very great evil. They could sincerely say like St Paul, "Woe to me if I preach not the gospel": Woe to me if I do not seek out vulgarity, superficiality, and false sentiment, and expose them wherever they lie hidden. A sincere inquisitor or a sincere witch-finder can hardly do his work with mildness. (*EIC* 125)

It is perhaps as well that Lewis did not name his opponents in the "Vigilant" more specifically. The "Leavisite" critic as a particular phenomenon of literary history may be long gone, but as a general type, "the Vigilant critic" lives on, though the evils requiring exposure would nowadays be different. The "usual suspects" of more recent years might include "monologism", "(phal)logocentrism" and "humanism".

However as Screwtape had pointed out, such fashion-dependent literary (or perhaps "cultural") scrupulosity is hardly compatible with *real* (as opposed to merely *theorized*) pleasure, and especially the pleasure of the text. As Lewis puts it in *An Experiment in Criticism*:

> Vigilance must already have prevented many happy unions of a good reader with a good book ... The all-important conjunction (Reader Meets Text) never seems to have been allowed to occur of itself and develop spontaneously. Here, plainly, are young people drenched, dizzied, and bedevilled by criticism to a point at which primary literary experience is no longer possible. (*EIC* 127-129)

Or in the rather more colourful terms of A.D. Nuttall, a great admirer of C. S. Lewis: "The final result may be a kind of literary teaching which crushes literary enjoyment, the natural *coitus* of reader and work endlessly *interruptus*."[8]

Like "the Enemy" in *The Screwtape Letters*, Lewis the reader is "a hedonist at heart". He has no problems with founding his theory of literature on pleasure. It is just that "pleasure" is an empty abstraction; the real work of defining the *particular* pleasure of reading still has to be done by a hedonistic theory of literature. Lewis resists locating the pleasure of the text in the "shape" or "form" of the *poiema* ("the something made" as opposed to the *logos*, "the something said"). Without explicitly mentioning the "Well-Wrought Urn" of Cleanth Brooks, Lewis nevertheless calls in

---

[8] A.D. Nuttall, *A New Mimesis,* (London: Methuen, 1983), p. 84.

question the adequacy of the metaphor of "shape" to the phenomenon of literature. "The parts of the Poiema are things we ourselves *do* ... in an order, and at a tempo, prescribed by the poet", he says (*EIC* 133; emphasis added). And "this is less like looking at a vase than like 'doing exercises' under an expert's direction or taking part in a choric dance invented by a good choreographer." (*EIC* 134) One wonders what Lewis would have made of Iser's phenomenological account of "the act of reading", which Lewis's approach seems in part to anticipate (Iser does mention some of Lewis's books, but I can find no reference by Iser to *An Experiment in Criticism*). What Lewis calls the distinctive literary pleasure of "obedience to what seems worth obeying and is not quite easily obeyed" (ibid.) is an end in itself, not a means to some further end, such as a view or philosophy of life, or a comment on life. (*EIC* 135) While Lewis rejects the literary theories of Aristotle and I.A. Richards, he thinks that they offer the right *sort* of theory; that is, "they place the goodness (where we actually feel it to be) in what has *happened* to us while we read" (ibid.; emphasis added).

The nearest Lewis gets to labelling what actually happens to us while we read is the phrase "an enlargement of our being" (*EIC* 137). "We want to be more than ourselves", he says; "we want to escape the illusions of perspective." (ibid.) By this Lewis does not mean that we aspire to some perspectiveless view, some objective "view from nowhere". Rather, "we want to see with other eyes, to imagine with other imaginations, to feel with other hearts, as well as our own." (ibid.) Here Lewis seems very close to the hermeneutical tradition, particularly perhaps to Gadamer; the latter says of the hermeneutical experience, paradigmatically the experience of reading, that it is experienced not "as a loss of self-possession, but rather as an *enrichment* of our self".[9] This resonance should not surprise us too much, since Lewis retained the imprint of his youthful Hegelianism long after most British philosophers had discarded such unfashionable views. And behind this quasi-Hegelian aesthetic is a Platonic impulse, of the kind expressed in modern times by Simone Weil and Iris Murdoch. Thus Lewis writes:

> The primary impulse of each is to maintain and aggrandize himself. The secondary impulse is to go out of the self, to correct its provincialism and heal its loneliness. In love, in virtue, in the pursuit of knowledge, and in the reception of the arts, we are doing this. Obviously this process can be described either as an enlargement or as a temporary annihilation of the

---

[9] Hans-Georg Gadamer, *Philosophical Hermeneutics* (Berkeley: University of California Press, 1977), p. 57; emphasis in original.

self. But that is an old paradox; "he that loseth his life shall save it". (*EIC* 138)

A key term in the above passage is "reception", which here means the good reading of good art and literature, rather than the mere "use" of bad art and literature "to maintain and aggrandize" the self (here Lewis is close to Iris Murdoch, especially in *The Fire and the Sun*[10]).

Lewis's residual Hegelianism is ultimately a form of Christian Platonism. The "stirb und werde" [die and become] motif runs through literary experience, love, moral action, and religion. There is no infinite qualitative difference, no absolute breach, between these central human experiences and Christian faith. Rather, there is a continuum from ordinary (but "real") pleasures to the bliss of the Beatific Vision. Lewis talks elsewhere of the "secret doctrine that *pleasures* are shafts of the glory as it strikes our sensibility".[11] Of such pleasures he writes:

> There need be no question of thanks or praise as a separate event, something done afterwards. To experience the tiny theophany is itself to adore.
> Gratitude exclaims, very properly: "How good of God to give me this." Adoration says: "What must be the quality of that Being whose far-off and momentary coruscations are like this!" One's mind runs back up the sunbeam to the sun.[12]

Such a "lived dialectic" is in effect a version of the ontological argument, as Lewis recognized when discussing "the dialectic of Desire" in the Preface to the Third Edition of *The Pilgrim's Regress*.[13] In this "lived dialectic", Sweet Desire, which "pierces us like a rapier at the smell of a bonfire, the sound of wild ducks flying overhead, the title of *The Well at the World's End*, the opening lines of *Kubla Khan*, the morning cobwebs in late summer, or the noise of falling waves", will, if diligently followed, lead in the end to the *real* object of desire, that is, to God.[14]

---

[10] Iris Murdoch, *The Fire and the Sun: Why Plato Banished the Artists* (based upon the Romanes Lecture 1976) (Oxford: Oxford University Press, 1977).

[11] C.S. Lewis, *Letters to Malcolm: Chiefly on Prayer* [1964] (London: Collins Fount, 1977), p.90. See also C.S. Lewis, *Selected Books* (London: HarperCollins, 2002), p. 28O.

[12] Ibid., pp. 91-2; see *Selected Books*, p. 281.

[13] C.S. Lewis, *The Pilgrim's Regress* [1933/1943] (London: Collins Fount, 1977), p. 15. See also *Selected Books* (London: HarperCollins, 2002), p. 9.

[14] Ibid.

While the pleasures that can lead us back to their divine source are by no means all literary, it is remarkable how many *are* literary, or have literary associations. One can see why Screwtape thinks that Wormwood has made a blunder of the first order by allowing his patient "to read a book he really enjoyed". But Wormwood's blunder pales into insignificance beside the incompetence of whatever devil was sent to acquire the soul of C. S. Lewis. For we discover that: "a fortnight before his death, he [Lewis] was reading *Les Liaisons Dangereuses* and writing to a colleague at Magdalene, Cambridge —'Wow, what a book!'"[15]

---

[15] A.N. Wilson, *C. S. Lewis: A Biography* (London: Collins, 1990), p.292.

CHAPTER SEVEN

THE LION, THE WITCH AND THE ATLANTEAN BOX: PSYCHOANALYSIS AND NARNIA REVISITED

However traumatic his reputed defeat at the hands of Elizabeth Anscombe in Oxford's Socratic Club in 1948 may (or may not) have been for C. S. Lewis[1], there is in his writings of the late 1940s and early 1950s a decisive shift away explicit apologetics, towards the quite different genre of the fairy-tale. Indeed, there was much in Lewis's life during these years[2] to drive him to seek the "recovery, escape and consolation" which Tolkien said were characteristic of the fairy-story.[3] In such circumstances the backless wardrobe (derived probably from E. Nesbit and George MacDonald) must have seemed like an escape-hatch. Whether we interpret such a resort to fairy-tale images in the face of stress as a form of "escapism", or as a sane and healthy response to a situation that had led in 1949 to Lewis's physical collapse, in fact it seems as if Lewis had little conscious control over the images; he says that they just came to him. In the case of *The Lion, the Witch and the Wardrobe* the images that came to him were "a faun carrying an umbrella, a queen on a sledge, [and] a magnificent lion". "At first," he adds, "there wasn't even anything

---

[1] For discussion of the debate between Lewis and Anscombe see R. E. Purtill, "Did C. S. Lewis Lose his Faith?" in Andrew Walker and James Patrick (eds), *A Christian for All Christians: Essays in Honour of C. S. Lewis* (London: Hodder and Stoughton, 1990); William Gray, *C. S. Lewis* (Northcote House, 1998), pp. 56-58; and Alan Jacobs, *The Narnian: The Life and Imagination of C.S. Lewis* (New York: HarperCollins, 2005), pp. 232-3. Jacobs plays down the impact of the "Anscombe affair", and criticizes the demonization of Anscombe as "the White Witch".

[2] See Gray, *C. S. Lewis*, p. 61.

[3] Tolkien, J.R.R, "On Fairy-stories" in *Tree and Leaf; Smith of Wootton Major; The Homecoming of Beorhtnoth* (London: Unwin, 1975), pp.57ff; see also *The Monsters and the Critics and Other Essays* (ed Christopher Tolkien) (London: HarperCollins, 2006), pp. 145ff. Hereafter cited in parentheses *MCOE*.

Christian about them."[4] As these images sorted themselves into events (i.e. became a story), they demanded a Form, and the Form that presented itself, and with which Lewis says he "fell in love", was that of the Fairy-Tale (*OTOW* 73). For Lewis a great advantage of the fairy-tale genre is that it circumvents the overly reverential attitude of conventional religious belief, which, he says, can "freeze feelings" and, with its lowered voices, make the whole business of religion seem "almost something medical" (ibid.). The fairy-tale form has an "inflexible hostility to all analysis, digression, reflections and 'gas'" (ibid.). The latter features are doubtless intended by Lewis to be seen as elements of the realist novel, but they might also perhaps be seen as characteristic of his own apologetic writing. But by casting his religious beliefs into an imaginary world, where vivid pictures are caught in the net of a fantastic narrative, might not some of these beliefs, Lewis asks, "appear in their real potency?" "Could one," he continues (and one has to wonder to what extent Elizabeth Anscombe is still at the back of his mind), "steal past those watchful dragons?" (*OTOW* 73)

But could there also be in the passage just quoted, with its references to "paralysing inhibitions" and "frozen feelings", to "lowered voices" in relation to "something medical", an echo of a much earlier trauma than the one Lewis may have experienced at the hands of Elizabeth Anscombe? Does the apparent loss of confidence in a familiar, stable world, which revolved around clever Jack the intellectual Giant-Killer, resonate with the much earlier loss of "all settled happiness, all that was tranquil and reliable", when his mother died?[5] The fairy-tale might not only allow Lewis to steal past an overly intellectualized and conventional kind of religion; it might also allow Jack to steal back to "the old security" of his original relationship with his mother, of which the later "stabs of Joy" are arguably the echoes. The essays on fairy-tales are full of the language of love and longing. As one of them says of a boy reading: "fairy land arouses a longing for he knows not what. It stirs and troubles him ... with the dim sense of something beyond his reach ... [T]he boy reading the fairy-tale desires and is happy in the very fact of desiring."[6] The Narnian

[4] C.S Lewis, "Sometimes Fairy Stories May Say Best What's to be Said", in *Of This and Other Worlds* (= U.S. *On Stories and Other Essays on Literature*) (ed. Walter Hooper) (London: Collins, 1982), p. 73. Hereafter cited in parentheses as *OTOW*.
[5] C.S. Lewis, *Surprised by Joy: The shape of my early life* [1955] (London: Collins Fontana, 1959), p. 23. Herafter cited in parentheses as *SBJ*.
[6] C.S Lewis, "On Three Ways of Writing for Children", *Of This and Other Worlds*, p. 65.

fairy-tales embody "the imaginary" not only in the conventional sense, but also in the psychoanalytical sense of the realm where the beginnings of the child's being and doing are played out in relation to its mother. *The Chronicles of Narnia* are over-determined in that they are *both* religiously motivated "allegories of love" à la Spenser (they are Lewis's "miniature *Faerie Queene*"), *and* unconsciously motivated "tales of love" à la Kristeva, where the self seeks the healing of a primal wound through the invocation and the evocation of the primary maternal matrix or *chora*.

The Lion, the Witch and the Wardrobe

Tolkien was critical of *The Chronicles of Narnia*, in part because they did not conform very closely to his criteria for "sub-creation". Nevertheless the Narnia stories do exhibit some of the main features of Tolkien's account of the fairy-story. Above all, they express the "joy" which is for Tolkien "the mark of the true fairy-story" (*MCOE* 155). Such joy is experienced in a "fleeting glimpse ... beyond the walls of the world, poignant as grief" (*MCOE* 153). It is particularly associated with the tale's sudden "turn" towards the Happy Ending or *eucatastrophe (*a word Tolkien coined): "In such stories when the sudden 'turn' comes we get a piercing glimpse of joy, and heart's desire, that for a moment passes outside the frame ... and lets a gleam come through." (*MCOE* 154)   A dramatic example of such a joyous "turn" comes in *The Lion, the Witch and the Wardrobe* when the Stone Table on which Aslan had been sacrificed cracks loudly, and the resurrected Aslan is suddenly standing behind Lucy and Susan, speaking to them. Tolkien calls such a glimpse of joy *evangelium* (good news or "gospel") and explicitly links it with what for him is the greatest fairy-tale of all: "The Gospels contain a fairy-story, or a story of a larger kind which embraces all the essence of fairy-stories." (*MCOE* 155)

If such a rewriting of the Gospel resurrection narratives scenes poses certain theological questions about Lewis's work,[7] there are also some psychological questions to be asked. After encountering the risen Aslan, Lucy has a momentary panic as she wonders whether Aslan might be a ghost. To reassure her, "Aslan stooped his golden head and licked her forehead. The warmth of his breath and a rich sort of smell that seemed to hang about his hair came all over her."[8] One does not have to swallow

---

[7] See William Gray, *C.S. Lewis,* p. 64.

[8] C.S. Lewis, *The Lion, the Witch and the Wardrobe* [1950] (London: HarperCollins, 1996), p. 147. Hereafter cited in parentheses as *LWW*.

everything in David Holbrook's *The Skeleton in the Wardrobe*[9] to feel that he is right to see in the children's experience with the resurrected Aslan the suggestion of a fantasy reconciliation between Lewis and his mother who died. Even if Lewis had not, as we shall see, spilled the beans in *The Magician's Nephew,* it would still have been tempting to read *The Chronicles of Narnia,* not only as a quest for Joy, but also as a quest for his lost mother. For Holbrook (who partly bases his thesis on Lewis's intense reaction to George MacDonald's quest for *his* lost mother in *Phantastes*), the trauma of Lewis's bereavement when he was nine years old reactivated an older and deeper sense of loss or lack somewhere in Lewis's earliest experience. Grounding his interpretation on Winnicott's view that play with the mother has a crucial role in fostering in the very young infant the beginnings of a sense of "being" and "reality", Holbrook postulates some kind of failure in Lewis's earliest environment. Unlike the case of George MacDonald where, remarkably, there actually is evidence of a traumatic weaning[10], there is in Lewis's case limited relevant biographical material, and Holbrook has to base his diagnosis largely on an ingenious reading of Lewis's fairy tales. Whatever we may make of some of Holbrook's more rebarbative translations of Lewis's fairy stories into psychoanalytical jargon, it is nevertheless hard entirely to dismiss his claim that something to do with the creative power of play in the "primary maternal matrix" is at work in, for example, the following description of a post-resurrection romp with Aslan:

> Laughing, though she didn't know why, Lucy scrambled over to reach him. Aslan leaped again. A mad chase began. Round and round the hill-top he led them, now hopelessly out of their reach, now letting them almost catch his tail, now diving between them, now tossing them in the air with his huge and beautifully velveted paws and catching them again, and now stopping unexpectedly so that all three of them rolled over together in a happy laughing heap of fur and arms and legs. (*LWW* 148-9)

To the obvious question of how such a *male* figure as Aslan can be associated with the mother, one answer might be that in the earliest pre-oedipal scenario "objects" (that is, "persons") have not yet been fully constituted, let alone gendered. For the very young infant, the mother is an "environment" rather than a person—thus Lucy cannot decide whether the romp is "more like playing with a thunderstorm or playing with a kitten"

---

[9] David Holbrook, *The Skeleton in the Wardrobe: C.S. Lewis' Fantasies: A Phenomenological Study* (Lewisburg: Bucknell University Press, 1991).
[10] See William Gray, "George Macdonald, Julia Kristeva and the Black Sun" note 6 above.

(*LWW* 148). Another, more controversial, response would be to invoke Julia Kristeva's notion of "the imaginary father".[11] Aslan seems to oscillate between, on the one hand, a playful and intimately tactile figure who evokes Kristeva's notion of "the semiotic"—at his very name "each one of the children felt something jump in its inside" (*LWW* 65); and, on the other, a terrifying and potentially punitive figure who, immediately after the romp just described, tells the girls to stop their ears because he intends to roar (*LWW* 149). In my view Holbrook greatly exaggerates what he calls the minatory or threatening aspect of Aslan, which he derives from the bullying and insane headmaster of "Belsen", as Lewis's preparatory school is called in *Surprised by Joy*. However, as I have discussed elsewhere,[12] the Chronicles do contain some worryingly cruel (even sadistic) scenes with Aslan.

Of the threatening quality of the White Witch, however, there can be no doubt. For Holbrook the Witch is the lost mother whose death is to the child the ultimate gesture of abandonment and rejection. Certainly the motif of the land frozen in perpetual winter, where it is "always winter and never Christmas", is a powerful symbol for the emotional death wrought by the rejecting and possibly hostile aspect of the dead mother. But it is only an *aspect* of the lost mother. The mother does not yet exist as a whole person for the very young child, according to the "object-relations" theory of D.W Winnicott and Melanie Klein; "she" is split into "part objects", which may, or may not, be integrated into a "whole object" to which the child, by growing into a "whole object" (i.e. by becoming a self), can begin to relate. The suggestion is that for Lewis the trauma of his mother's death exacerbated some already existing failure properly to integrate the "parts" of "himself" and his mother into viable selves. In technical terms, it has been suggested, Lewis remained stuck in Klein's "paranoid-schizoid" position, with the Witch representing the terrifyingly cruel and rejecting Bad Mother (or "Breast"), and Aslan representing (for at least some of the time) the ultimately satisfying and desirable Good Mother (or "Breast"). Kristeva seems to be saying something quite similar to Klein and Winnicott, though in different terms, when she talks of the "abjection" of the mother. The "abject" is the abjected mother; it is terrifying, uncanny and repulsive, precisely because it transgresses any defining limits which might stabilize and secure a human identity. It is paradigmatically the "undead", or the vampire; one of the clearest examples in literature of the

---

[11] See Julia Kristeva, *Tales of Love* (New York: Columbia University Press, 1987), p.46; William Gray, *C.S Lewis*, p.66; and "Death, Myth and Reality in C. S. Lewis" above.
[12] William Gray, *C.S Lewis*, pp. 73; 80f.

"abject" is George MacDonald's Lilith.[13] Significantly the White Witch is not human, though she appears to be; as Mr. Beaver tells the children, she is a daughter of Lilith, not of Eve (*LWW* 76). Mr. Beaver continues in a passage that is genuinely disturbing:

> But there's no two views about things that look like humans and aren't ... take my advice, and when you meet anything that's going to be human and isn't yet, or used to be human once and isn't now, or ought to be human and isn't, you keep your eyes on it and feel for your hatchet. (*LWW* 77)

Terrifying as the Witch may be, it is even more terrifying to find an exemplar of "live and let live" decency exhibiting such ferocious paranoia. This is the violence which is truly unsettling in *The Lion, the Witch and the Wardrobe*, and not the mildly realistic battle scenes to which Holbrook rather moralistically objects.

The Magician's Nephew

In *The Magician's Nephew* the presence of Digory's dying mother is pervasive. Between the introduction in chapter one of the tear-stained boy whose mother is dying, and the moment in chapter eleven when Digory finally asks Aslan for something "to make Mother well", there are regular reminders (at least ten) of his mother's frail condition. Thus, despite momentous events such as the death and birth of worlds (Charn and Narnia respectively), the reader is never allowed to forget what the story is really about. Lewis could hardly make it clearer that the birth of Narnia is intimately connected with his attempt somehow to come to terms with the death of his mother.

Lewis locates the beginning of *The Magician's Nephew* in Edwardian London—the world of Sherlock Holmes and E. Nesbit's Bastable children; and also of course the world of the young Jack Lewis. Digory's father is abroad, but his Uncle Andrew, far from acting as a good father-substitute for Digory, is cruel, vain and dangerous, being something of a magician. Digory is thrown back on the support of the girl next door, Polly Plummer. Together they accidentally stumble into Uncle Andrew's secret chamber, where Uncle Andrew makes Polly disappear by means of a magic ring, thus compelling Digory to follow her with the ring that will bring them home. Before Digory leaves to follow Polly, he is given the history of the rings. Uncle Andrew had inherited from a Mrs Lefay, who was literally his

---

[13] See my "The Angel in the House of Death: Gender and Subjectivity in George MacDonald's *Lilith*" reprinted above.

fairy-godmother, a box which, it transpired, was of Atlantean origin. Atlantis is of course significant for Lewis in that the loss of security he suffered at his mother's death is described in *Surprised by Joy* as being like the sinking of the great continent of Atlantis (*SBJ* 23). In a phrase which suggests far more than its literal meaning, Uncle Andrew says: "The Atlantean box contained something that had been brought from another world when our world was only just beginning."[14] On a literal level, the box contains dust from another world (actually from "the Wood between the Worlds") which Uncle Andrew has succeeded in making into magic rings. On a symbolic level "the Atlantean box" suggests the "primary maternal matrix" or Kristeva's semiotic *chora*, from which the beginnings of all human being and identity emerge.[15] *The Magician's Nephew* can be read as an account of Lewis's attempt, in the realm of the imaginary, to return to the primary maternal matrix from which he was "untimely ripp'd", and to find a new beginning in which that primary loss is more successfully dealt with.

When Digory puts on the ring, he finds himself in what he names "the Wood between the Worlds", an intermediate place of womb-like "dreamful ease", where he finds Polly and one of Uncle Andrew's guinea-pigs. The children decide to explore some of the other worlds that can be entered via the many pools in the Wood. Their first stop is the dead world of Charn, where Digory awakens the terrifying witch Jadis from an enchanted sleep. In psychoanalytical terms Jadis can be read as the "split-off" "Bad Mother", the epitome of rejecting cruelty. She is of course the White Witch of *The Lion, the Witch and the Wardrobe*, who embodies the feelings of rejection the young Lewis would most probably have had at his mother's death (and perhaps earlier, if Holbrook is right). After a bizarre interlude back in London, Jadis and the children, now accompanied by Uncle Andrew, a cabby, and a horse named Strawberry, find themselves in utter darkness, in a place "without form and void". There they witness the creation of the world of Narnia. It begins with a voice singing. The voice seems to come from all directions at once, and even out of the earth: "Its lower notes were deep enough to be the voice of the earth herself [sic]. There were no words. There was hardly even a tune. But it was, beyond comparison, the most beautiful noise he [Digory] had ever heard. It was so beautiful he could hardly bear it." (*MN* 93) As the Voice sings into

---

[14] C.S. Lewis, *The Magician's Nephew* [1955] (London: HarperCollins, 1996), p.25. Hereafter cited in parentheses as *MN*.
[15] On the "semiotic" and the "*chora*" see Julia Kristeva, *Revolution in Poetic Language* (trans. Margaret Waller) (New York: Columbia University Press, 1984); extracts in *The Kristeva Reader* (ed Toril Moi) (Oxford: Blackwell, 1986).

existence first stars, and then a sun, the children and the cabby can be seen with faces filled with joy, looking as if the sound "reminded them of something" (*MN* 94). While this scene clearly echoes the Biblical Creation myth, there are also eches of another myth of origins, that told by psychoanalysts such as Winnicott and Kristeva, where the individual comes into being in the play of the mother's voice and eyes and body. Lewis seems here to going back into "the semiotic", the living pulse of song, to find a new beginning with a good mother. This "good mother" is Aslan (his maleness notwithstanding). In a later passage which echoes the remarkable description of Lewis's first encounter with the "Holiness" of George MacDonald's *Phantastes*, experienced as an intangible, elusive presence connected with "the voice of my mother or my nurse" (*SBJ* 145), Lewis gives the following account of Aslan as the semiotic "Good Mother" (or "Imaginary Father"):

> Both the children were looking up into the Lion's face ... and all at once ... the face seemed to be a sea of tossing gold in which they were floating, and such a sweetness and power rolled about them and over them and entered them that they felt that they had never been happy or wise or good, or even alive and awake, before. And the memory of that moment stayed with them always, so that ... if ever they were sad or afraid or angry, the thought of all that golden goodness, and the feeling that it was still there, quite close, just around some corner or just behind some door, would come back and make them sure, deep down inside, that all was well. (*MN* 165)

At the end of the book Digory finally dares to approach Aslan to ask for something to cure his dying mother. Aslan shares Digory's grief, but promises nothing. Instead he sets Digory the task of bringing him an apple from a tree in the garden at the Western end of the World. When Digory reaches the garden and plucks the apple of life, he encounters the Witch, who tempts him to take it to his dying mother:

> "Soon she will be well again. All will be well again. Your home will be happy again. You will be like other boys."
> "Oh!" gasped Digory as if he had been hurt, and put his hand to his head. For he now knew that the most terrible choice lay before him. (*MN* 150)

Obedience for its own sake, against all that seems reasonable and humane, is required of Digory; it seems that he must accept the inevitability of his mother's death. This is a reenactment of Lewis's childhood trauma, when he had to come to terms with the fact that that his prayers for his mother's recovery remained unanswered. In this reprise of Lewis's own early experience, Digory comes to accept that "there might be things more terrible than losing someone you love by death" (*MN* 163). But although Digory wins through to acceptance, he is spared the ultimate trial which the young Lewis had to face. Aslan tells him to pluck an apple which *will* heal his mother. For Digory "it is as if the whole world had turned inside out and upside down." (*MN* 163) This is the "joyous turn", the *eucatastrophe*, which Tolkien demanded of the fairy-tale, and which brings consolation to the reader (*MCOE* 153). What kind of consolation this imaginary resolution may have brought to the writer is another question.

The Last Battle

The Last Battle is a profoundly melancholy book. It opens with a depressing vignette of domestic tyranny in which the ruthless ape Shift routinely exploits the good will and gullibility of Puzzle the donkey. Whatever traces it may contain of Lewis's own reputed domestic bondage to Mrs Moore, this opening chapter also anticipates the apocalyptic conclusion of *The Last Battle* when, in the words of the poet Lewis wished to emulate:

> The ceremony of innocence is drowned;
> The best lack all conviction, while the worst
> Are full of passionate intensity.[16]

By the second chapter we are warned that: "there have not been such disastrous conjunctions of the planets for five hundred years ... [S]ome great evil hangs over Narnia."[17]

Then "a really dreadful thing" happens. Tirian and Jewel come across two Calormenes whipping a Talking Horse; enraged, they kill the Calormenes without warning. Tirian feels that he is dishonoured, and must surrender himself to be brought before Aslan. He realizes that he is going to his death, but asks: "Would it not be better to be dead than to have this horrible fear that Aslan has come and it is not like the Aslan we believed in and longed for? It is as if the sun rose one day and were a black sun." *(LB* 29) This echoes the image of "the black sun of melancholy" in Gerard de Nerval's poem "El Desdichado" [the disinherited one], which Julia Kristeva takes for the title of her book *Black Sun: Depression and*

---

[16] W.B. Yeats, "The Second Coming"
[17] C.S. Lewis, *The Last Battle* [1956] (London: HarperCollins, 1996), p. 19. Hereafter cited in parentheses as *LB*.

Melancholia. Whether or not Lewis knew Nerval's poem, he would certainly have encountered the "black sun" image in George MacDonald's *Phantastes*.[18] Kristeva's analysis of the melancholy inscribed in Nerval's poem seems to fit Lewis's life and work uncannily well. The prince in Nerval's poem is disinherited not of a "property" or "object", but of "an unnameable domain ...the secret and unreachable horizon of our loves and desires ... [which] assumes, for the imagination, the consistency of an archaic mother."[19] The loss that is really being mourned in *The Last Battle* is not so much that of Narnia as that of Atlantis, the "archaic mother", whose sinking has caused Lewis inconsolable grief. As Kristeva puts it: "The melancholy does not pass. Neither does the poet's past."[20]

The Last Battle depicts a losing battle against despair. Hope keeps reviving, but only to be dashed. Finally Narnia falls, due in large measure to the villainy of the dwarfs. If ever anything was, to use Tolkien's term, a "*dyscatastrophe*", this is it. It seems the end of Narnia, and of all the joy it has brought. But in a final turn of "sudden and miraculous grace", *dyscatastrophe* is turned into "the joy of deliverance", a deliverance which "denies (in the face of much evidence, if you will) universal final defeat and in so far is *evangelium* [good news], giving a fleeting glimpse of Joy, Joy beyond the walls of the world, poignant as grief." (*MCOE* 153) But this turn to Joy is to be no brief encounter. For the stable into which the friends of Narnia are forced at the end of the battle contains Heaven itself, Aslan's country. In a reprise of Lucy's first experience in the wardrobe, it turns out that "its inside is bigger than its outside". But this time it seems it cannot be Narnia that is through the door, because the door leads *from* Narnia into somewhere else, which is nevertheless strangely reminiscent of Narnia. As Professor Digory Kirke realizes, this is in Platonic terms "the real Narnia", of which the vanished Narnia was only the shadow or copy. The company of true Narnians rushes ever "further up and further in" into ever more real Narnias (*LB* 159-61).

This journey from glory to glory, ever further up and further in, embodies the vision of Christian Platonism. Its theological adequacy must be discussed elsewhere. The question that concerns us here is whether, in this very grand finale, the broken heart of the boy from Belfast is finally

---

[18] See Chapter One above, "George MacDonald, Julia Kristeva and the Black Sun".

[19] Julia Kristeva, *Black Sun: Depression and Melancholia* (New York: Columbia University Press, 1989), p.145.

[20] Julia Kristeva, *Black Sun*, p. 165.

mended.[21] That boy haunts the pages of *The Chronicles of Narnia*, until at the end of *The Magician's Nephew* his mother is restored to life by the goodness of Aslan and the power of Narnian magic. But in *The Last Battle* the goodness of Aslan is called in question, and Narnia itself falls. The main doubters of Aslan and his goodness are the dwarfs, who are also pivotal in the fall of Narnia. They too come through the stable door, but refuse to believe in the wonderful new world which the friends of Narnia find. For them, it is simply a pathetic illusion. For them, there is no "healing of harms". For them, the children's vision of their dead mother and father waving to them across the valley, as if "from the deck of a big ship when you are waiting on the quay" (*LB* 170), would be just one more piece of wishful thinking. It would be "all that stuff about family reunions 'on the further shore' ... out of bad hymns and lithographs ... it rings false. We *know* it couldn't be like that."[22] The voice here, of course, is not that of the dwarfs, but of the narrator of *A Grief Observed*. It seems that the dwarfs (or manikins[23], as they are sometimes called) are never entirely left behind.

However the presence of the dwarfs or manikins in the "real Narnia" is not merely some stubborn hangover from an older, fallen order. Rather it grounds, and perhaps guarantees, the reality of the new order, and prevents the wonderful new creation from being mere fantasy. Perhaps it was only by expressing and containing his melancholy that Lewis could begin to come to terms with it. Winnicott has argued that depression is actually an *achievement*[24] which leads beyond the so-called "paranoid-schizoid" position; to accept depression enables one to get in touch with reality. It is noticeable that in Lewis's late work there is a subtly different "taste" to his spirituality. Far from his "bonny fighter" days as the star of Oxford's Socratic Club, there is in the late Lewis a maturity and a gentleness which have much to do with a greater capacity to tolerate loss and ambiguity. As Winnicott suggests, "letting go" is only really possible on the basis of

---

[21] The original context of this paper was the Lewis Centenary conference in Belfast.

[22] C.S. Lewis, *A Grief Observed* [published under the pseudonym N.W. Clerk 1961; reprinted under Lewis's name in 1964] (London: Faber Paperbacks, 1966), p. 23.

[23] The term "manikin" may recall the "part objects" of "object relations theory", and even perhaps Lacan's "*l'hommelette*" (see *The Four Fundamental Concepts of Psychoanalysis: The Seminar of Jacques Lacan, Book XI* (Jacques-Alain Miller (ed.); Alan Sheridan (trans.)) (New York: Norton, 1998). p. 197.

[24] D.W. Winnicott, *The Maturational Process and the Facilitating Environment* (London: Hogarth, 1965). pp. 73-82.

having been satisfactorily "held". And towards the end of his life, Jack Lewis had in every sense found, and been found by, Joy.

CHAPTER EIGHT

PULLMAN, LEWIS, MACDONALD AND THE ANXIETY OF INFLUENCE

"Just as we can never embrace … a single person, but embrace the whole of her or his family romance, so we can never read a poet without reading the whole of his or her family romance as a poet."[1]

Introduction

The present essay began life as an attempt to explore the possible relationship between the fantasy writing of Philip Pullman and that of George MacDonald. However, that attempt rapidly encountered the force of Harold Bloom's warning against the error of treating poets as if they were self-contained individuals. In *The Anxiety of Influence* Bloom is admittedly making specific reference to the relations between lyric poets, whereas the work to be discussed in the present chapter is fantasy writing in prose. Nevertheless I believe that Bloom's analysis of the "family romances" of "poets as poets" can be adapted to apply to writers in other literary genres, and to the so-to-speak "familial" relations that constitute a writer as a creative literary individual. Indeed, Bloom himself sought in his 1980 paper "*Clinamen*: Towards a Theory of Fantasy" to apply his "anxiety of influence" theory not only to the genealogy of the literary *genre* (or rather sub-genre[2]) of fantasy, but also to the relationships between particular instances of fantasy writing, for example the relation of his own *The Flight to Lucifer* to David Lindsay's *A Voyage to Arcturus*. Of course the gender bias of Bloom's famous theory of "the anxiety of influence" was long ago pointed out by Sandra Gilbert and Susan Gubar in

---

[1] Harold Bloom, *The Anxiety of Influence: A Theory of Poetry* (New York: Oxford University Press, 1973), p. 94.
[2] Harold Bloom, "*Clinamen*: Towards a Theory of Fantasy" in E. Slusser, E. Rabkin and R. Scholes (eds), *Bridges to Fantasy* Carbondale: Southern Illinois University Press, 1982), p. 2.

their *The Madwoman in the Attic*.[3] This is an issue to which I shall return later in this essay. What I hope to show in the present chapter that however tenuous and complex the "family" connections that link Pullman and MacDonald may be, they tend to be dominated by another figure who is closely and inextricably associated with both of them: C.S. Lewis. Lewis figures, firstly, as a bad father to Pullman, a seemingly inevitable precursor whose writing seems to fascinate as well as repel Pullman. Secondly, Lewis appears as MacDonald's dutiful son, devoted to his spiritual (if not literary) master. Ultimately, however, there seems to me to be something hollow and unconvincing about both these versions of a filial relationship. In the first place, Lewis is arguably not the moral monster that Pullman makes him out to be; and secondly, MacDonald is more than just the spiritual director (important as that is) that Lewis presents us with. For one thing, MacDonald is, I will argue, a much better writer than Lewis would have us believe. While there is not necessarily any "taint of insincerity" in these misrepresentations, only perhaps something rather *voulu* (as Owen Barfield once said of C.S. Lewis[4]), nevertheless Pullman and Lewis could also be seen as "framing" their precursors, in all the senses of Barbara Johnson's memorable usage of the term "frame"[5]. However, it is Harold Bloom's "map of misreading", in its own way as arcane as Johnson's poststructuralist subtleties, which seems more apt here, and more in tune with the Gnostic sympathies of both Pullman and MacDonald.

Without venturing too far into the battery of explicitly Gnostic categories that Bloom elaborates in *The Anxiety of Influence* and *A Map of Misreading*[6], one might suggest that it is the first two of his six strategies for misreading—or "revisionary ratios", as Bloom calls them—that might seem to apply most readily to the relationships that are the subject of the present paper. *Clinamen* (or "swerving") might arguably apply to the relation of Philip Pullman and C.S. Lewis, with the former "swerving"

---

[3] Sandra M. Gilbert and Susan Gubar, *The Madwoman in the Attic: The Woman Writer and the Nineteenth-Century Literary Imagination* (New Haven: Yale University Press, 1979), pp. 46-51.

[4] Owen Barfield in the Introduction to Jocelyn Gibb (ed.), *Light on C.S. Lewis* (London: Geoffrey Bles, 1965) p. xi. See also William Gray, *C.S. Lewis* (Plymouth: Northcote House, 1998), p. 5.

[5] Barbara Johnson's "The Frame of Reference", which has been reprinted in various collections, first appeared in the special issue on "Literature and Psychoanalysis" of *Yale French Studies* 55/56, 1977.

[6] Harold Bloom, *A Map of Misreading* (New York: Oxford University Press, 1975).

away from his precursor in a corrective movement. Bloom's second "revisionary ratio" *tessera* (or "antithetical completion") might seem more appropriate to the way in which C.S. Lewis (as we hope to show below) "antithetically completes his precursor, by so reading [MacDonald's work] as to retain its terms but to mean them in another sense, as though the precursor had failed to go far enough."[7] However, Bloom's six "revisionary ratios" are so general—Bloom himself is quite undogmatic about their number, their names and their application—that it is difficult to be very precise in applying them. In the context of the present discussion of MacDonald, Lewis and Pullman, I propose simply to use Bloom's general idea that a writer must necessarily *misread* a significant precursor in order to achieve his own identity as a writer. Gilbert and Gubar have argued (referring *en passant* to MacDonald's *Lilith*) that *The Anxiety of Influence* depends on a patriarchal Oedipal scenario.[8] While I intend to argue that there is a degree of Bloomian misreading involved both in the relationship of Pullman to C.S. Lewis, and of Lewis to George MacDonald, I also intend ultimately to retain a degree of suspicion towards the Oedipal focus of Bloom's approach.

Pullman explicitly gives his own version of his literary origins in the "Acknowledgements" that conclude the *His Dark Materials* trilogy. He writes: "I have stolen ideas from every book I have ever read. My principle in researching for a novel is 'Read like a butterfly, write like a bee', and if this story contains any honey, it is entirely because of the quality of the nectar I found in the work of better writers."[9] While this description smacks rather more of free love than of the obsessive Oedipal conflicts of the Bloomian nuclear family, there is nevertheless an interestingly masculinist subtext to its intertext. The phrase "Float like a butterfly, sting like a bee" originated of course with Muhammed Ali (the boxer formerly known as Cassius Clay), than whom a stronger expression of male self-creation through conflict would be hard to find—with Sonny Liston figuring as the Bad Daddy in this Oedipal psychodrama. The suggestion that Pullman is, like Ali, "the Greatest" is reinforced by the quotations on the covers of Pullman's books: "Is [Philip Pullman] the best storyteller ever?" and "Move over Tolkien and C.S. Lewis…" Admittedly this "hype" does not necessarily reflect Pullman's own views, though the extraordinarily ambitious scope of *His Dark Materials* has not escaped

---

[7] Harold Bloom, *The Anxiety of Influence* (New York: Oxford University Press, 1973), p. 14.

[8] Gilbert and Gubar, loc. cit.

[9] Philip Pullman, *The Amber Spyglass* (London: Scholastic, 2000), p. 549. Hereafter cited in parentheses as *AS*.

some critical suspicions of hubris.[10] Pullman is by any standards a "strong" poet or writer, and one unafraid of flaunting his literary lineage. Though Pullman himself has been in some respects critical of postmodernism[11], some critics have found in his work an (inter)textually promiscuous postmodern pluralism.[12] Such postmodern intertextual promiscuity notwithstanding, there is nevertheless one figure with whom it seems Pullman must contend above all others, and that is C.S. Lewis. This encounter seems susceptible of a Bloomian interpretation as an Oedipal misreading of a literary father figure.

Philip Pullman and C.S. Lewis

Pullman has frequently and publicly attacked C.S Lewis, most notoriously perhaps in his article "The Dark Side of Narnia" which vilifies the "pernicious" Narnia series as "one of the most ugly and poisonous things I've ever read" on account of "the misogyny, the racism, the sado-masochistic relish for violence that permeates it".[13] While none of these charges against Lewis is new, or entirely unfounded perhaps, it is in fact the "relish for violence that permeates" *Pullman's attack on Lewis* that is most striking. Lewis seems too close to Pullman for the latter's comfort. Pullman clearly feels the need to distinguish his own work from what seems to the innocent eye to be the rather similar work of Lewis. Specific textual correspondences could be multiplied: for example, in the first book of both the *His Dark Materials* trilogy and *The Chronicles of Narnia* the heroine makes a momentous discovery in a wardrobe (even the names "Lyra" and "Lucy" are not too dissimilar—Blake's "Lyca"[14] notwithstanding). However, it is the general thematic similarities that are most striking: both Pullman and Lewis have written fantasy with a

---

[10] Erica Wagner, quoted in Claire Squires, *Philip Pullman's His Dark Materials' Trilogy* (London: Continuum, 2004), p. 74.
[11] Pullman has said in discussion with Rowan Williams that he is "temperamentally ... 'agin' the postmodernist position that there is no truth and it depends on where you are and it's all the result of the capitalist, imperialist hegemony of bourgeois ... all this sort of stuff". See Lyn Haill (ed.), *Darkness Illuminated* (London: National Theatre / Oberon Books, 2004), p. 101.
[12] For example Deborah Cogan Thacker and Jean Webb, *Introducing Children's Literature: from Romanticism to Postmodernism* (London: Routledge, 2002), pp. 148; 151-6.
[13] Philip Pullman, "The Dark Side of Narnia", *The Guardian,* October 1, 1998; quoted in Squires, op. cit., p. 17.
[14] See "The Little Girl Lost" and "The Little Girl Found" in *Songs of Experience.*

religious (or quasi-religious) angle about growing up, with lots of intertextual allusions. If Pullman in an interview has called the *His Dark Materials* trilogy "*Paradise Lost* for teenagers in three volumes"[15], then Lewis's *The Silver Chair* has been called "*The Faerie Queene* in miniature".[16] Of course, according to Pullman, his fantasy is not really fantasy, though his claim in the same interview that *Northern Lights* is "not fantasy ...[but] a work of stark realism"[17] seems to be somewhat tenuously based on his alleged superiority over the likes of Tolkien in the portrayal of psychology. Pullman is apparently anti-religious, though Hugh Rayment-Pickard in *The Devil's Account: Philip Pullman and Christianity* does not have to work very hard to disengage Pullman's "hidden theology". Rayment-Pickard forbears from any accusation of disingenuousness on Pullman's part, suggesting only that the latter's claim not to have a "message", being merely a story-teller, is a kind of blind spot.[18] Pullman clearly does have a "message" that is in certain crucial respects different from Lewis's Christian one; however, the practical moral outcomes seem *mutatis mutandis* pretty similar, as is evident in the following passage from *The Amber Spyglass* where the angel Xaphania offers Will and Lyra these words of wisdom:

> "Conscious beings make Dust—they renew it all the time, by thinking and feeling and reflecting, by gaining wisdom and passing it on. And if you help everyone else in your worlds to do that, by helping them to learn and understand about themselves and each other and the way everything works, and by showing how to be kind instead of cruel, and patient instead of hasty, and cheerful instead of surly, and above all how to keep their minds open and free and curious ..." (*AS* 520)

Evidently Lewis has no monopoly on preaching, for Pullman shows himself here to be just as capable of didacticism as the next children's author.

The real sites of conflict between Pullman and Lewis in this Oedipal struggle are, unsurprisingly, sex and death. Pullman specifically takes issue with two scenes in Lewis's *The Last Battle*. Firstly, he criticises

---

[15] Wendy Parsons and Catriona Nicholson, "Talking to Philip Pullman: An Interview", *The Lion and the Unicorn* 23: 1 January 1999; quoted in Squires, op. cit., p. 17.

[16] Doris T. Myers, *C.S. Lewis in Context* (Kent, Ohio: Kent State University Press, 1994), p. 157.

[17] Squires, op. cit., p. 17.

[18] Hugh Rayment-Pickard, *The Devil's Account: Philip Pullman and Christianity* (London: Darton Longman and Todd, 2004), p. 23.

Lewis for excluding Susan from "the real Narnia", or Heaven, on account of her being "interested in nothing nowadays except nylons and lipstick and invitations".[19] This passage is often seen as some kind of sexist and/or puritan and/or misogynist attack on female sexuality, for which the nylons and lipstick and invitations are metonyms. Pullman accuses Lewis of a kind of prudish condemnation of adolescent sexuality, which he by contrast seeks to celebrate in the scene at the end of *The Amber Spyglass* where Will and Lyra mutually stroke their demons' fur, an activity that presumably refers metonymically to some kind of sexual intimacy. However, I feel that Lewis has perhaps been rather harshly treated on this issue. The problem with Susan is not so much her adolescent sexuality as such, but the fact that she allows the *construction* of that sexuality to be so all absorbing that she doesn't *want* anything else. And you don't have to be sexist and/or puritan and/or misogynist to worry about what our culture does to teenage girls. When Lyra and Will begin to explore their sexuality, they are still involved in a heroic quest; that's precisely what Susan— sadly—doesn't seem to want anymore.

Secondly, Pullman criticises Lewis for his allegedly "horrible" message that being killed in a train crash is the best thing ever if you end up in Heaven.[20] Apart from the fact that *His Dark Materials* is at least as violent as anything that Lewis ever wrote, Lewis's Platonism by no means necessarily implies a devaluation, let alone a hatred, of this world, only some care in our dealings with it. There is always a danger of conflating Platonism and Manichaeism. The latter *is* precisely world-hating, since for it Creation is actually the Fall, and consequently the world and the flesh are merely snares (or indeed "tombs") from which the Manichaean adept seeks only escape—though not just yet, as one famous ex-Manichaean once pleaded![21] That famous ex-Manichaean, St Augustine of Hippo, was acutely aware of the importance of discriminating between on the one hand Manichaeism, which despite the claims of its adherents was profoundly anti-Christian; and on the other hand Platonism, which was in Augustine's mature view compatible with Christian faith, though of course insufficient on its own.[22] C.S. Lewis stands in a long line of Christian Platonists for whom the world and the body are, as the good creations of a

---

[19] C.S. Lewis, *The Last Battle* (London: HarperCollins, 1997), p. 128.
[20] Pullman interview with Susan Roberts for Christian Aid, quoted in Rayment-Pickard, op. cit., p. 45.
[21] St Augustine of Hippo, *Confessions* 8:7.
[22] On Augustine, Platonism and Manichaeism see above all Peter Brown, *Augustine of Hippo* (London: Faber, 1967). See also Elaine Pagels, *Adam, Eve and the Serpent* (Harmondsworth: Penguin, 1990), chapter 6 passim.

good God, capable of expressing divine beauty and wisdom. That human beings are perennially prone to idolize, degrade and exploit that which if used properly should reflect the glory of God, is the problem of sin or evil. The point is that Christian Platonism, far from being world-hating, wants the world and the body to be used in the right way, that is, as images of the divine life. In this sense it is deeply world-affirming. The difficulty is that Platonism, like Christian faith itself, is dialectical, since the very desire that leads ultimately to God is dangerously powerful and always prone to short-circuiting the spiritual (and not only the spiritual) system by seeking premature fulfilment or joy. And joy prematurely grasped inevitably turns out to be mere pleasure or "thrills". All of this is made abundantly clear in Lewis's deeply Augustinian spiritual autobiography, *Surprised by Joy*.[23]

Pullman, then, is perfectly entitled to proclaim some kind of this-worldly message; however, firstly, it is not the case that in order to do so he has necessarily to misread Lewis as a quasi-Manichaean (though a Bloomian reading might claim precisely that he *does* have to); and secondly, Pullman's purported this-worldliness appears less than consistent. It seems rather odd, for example, that a self-proclaimed this-worldly atheist should allow any sort of post-mortem existence whatsoever, as in the world of the dead sequence in *The Amber Spyglass* when, in a kind of reversal of the Orpheus and Eurydice myth, Lyra goes to find and rescue her friend Roger who has been captured and killed by "the Gobblers". More significantly, the ghosts escaping from the world of the dead (which incidentally seems to owe something to the conclusion of Ursula Le Guin's *The Farthest Shore*) are seen to achieve a kind of blissful release in a moment of mystic pantheism that is again rather hard to reconcile with a rigorous this-worldly atheism. As Lyra reassures the ghosts, reading the alethiometer:

> "But your daemons en't just *nothing* now; they're part of everything. All the atoms that were them, they've gone into the air and the wind and the trees and the earth and all the living things. They'll never vanish. They're just part of everything. And that's exactly what'll happen to you …" (*AS* 335)

One of the ghosts takes up Lyra's theme: "[W]e'll be alive again in a thousand blades of grass, and a million leaves, we'll be falling in the raindrops and blowing in the fresh breeze, we'll be glittering in the dew under the stars and the moon …" *(AS* 336) And when the ghost of Lyra's

---

[23] C.S. Lewis, *Surprised by Joy* (London: Fontana, 1959). See also the chapter "The Quest for Joy (or the Dialectic of Desire)" in Gray, *C.S. Lewis*, pp. 4-16.

old friend Roger becomes the first to achieve release from the world of the dead, it is presented as a moment of intoxication:

> He took a step forward, and turned to look back at Lyra, and laughed in surprise as he found himself turning into the night, the starlight, the air … and then he was gone, leaving behind such a vivid little burst of happiness that Will was reminded of the bubbles in a glass of champagne. (*AS* 382)

Pullman at this point seems very close, *mutatis mutandis*, to the Romantic pantheism of Wordsworth, for example as it is expressed—admittedly with much more ambiguity and ambivalence than Pullman's "Happy Hour" version of pantheistic mystical surrender—in "A slumber did my spirit seal":

> No motion has she now, no force;
>   She neither hears nor sees;
> Rolled round in earth's diurnal course,
>   With rocks, and stones, and trees.

There is even a hint in Pullman's text at this point of something not dissimilar to MacDonald's notion of the "good death'" which the young Lewis picked up on.[24] The "good death" motif is in part a version of the Romantic principle of "stirb und werde" [die and become]; it is perhaps most strangely expressed in the flying fish which dives into the boiling pot in *The Golden Key*—the latter is incidentally the only MacDonald text that Pullman says he actually remembers reading.[25] Perhaps there lies, behind Pullman's inconsistent (but in a Bloomian sense necessary) misreading of Lewis, a family resemblance to the literary father that Lewis in his turn misread, George MacDonald.

C.S. Lewis and George MacDonald

If Pullman's misreading of Lewis is an act of vilification, Lewis's misreading of MacDonald is an act of sanctification. Lewis claimed MacDonald as his spiritual master, and famously said: "I fancy I have never written a book in which I did not quote from him." (*GMA* 20) For Lewis, MacDonald was "the greatest genius" as a maker of myths, and of "fantasy that hovers between the allegorical and the mythopoeic" (*GMA*

---

[24] C.S. Lewis, *George MacDonald: An Anthology* (London: Bles, 1946), p. 21. Hereafter cited in parentheses as *GMA*.
[25] Personal correspondence (2005).

16; 14). However, Lewis did not rate MacDonald as a writer; in literary terms MacDonald was, according to Lewis, not even second-rate:

> In making these extracts I have been concerned with MacDonald not as a writer but as a Christian teacher. If I were to deal with him as a writer, as a man of letters, I would be faced with a difficult critical problem. If we define Literature as an art whose medium is words, then certainly MacDonald has no place in its first rank— perhaps not even in its second. There are indeed passages ... where the wisdom and (I would dare to call it) the holiness that are in him triumph over and even burn away the baser elements in his style: the expression becomes precise, weighty, economic; acquires a cutting edge. But he does not maintain this level for long. The texture of his writing as a whole is undistinguished, at times fumbling. Bad pulpit traditions cling to it; there is sometimes a nonconformist verbosity, sometimes an old Scotch weakness for florid ornament ... sometimes an over-sweetness picked up from Novalis. (*GMA* 14)

It is noteworthy that even those elements of MacDonald's style that do not offend Lewis's highly sensitive critical palate are attributed to the holiness of MacDonald the Christian teacher, rather than to the skill of MacDonald the professional writer. Lewis's assertion that "the texture of [MacDonald's] writing *as a whole* is undistinguished"[26] seems to disallow the move which would interpret his criticisms of MacDonald's writing style as applying only to the "realist" novels, but not to the fantasy works. Lewis does make a sharp qualitative distinction between the two bodies of MacDonald's work: "[MacDonald's] great works are *Phantastes*, the *Curdie* books, *The Golden Key*, *The Wise Woman*, and *Lilith* ... [T]hey are supremely good in their own kind ... The meaning, the suggestion, the radiance, is incarnate in the whole story..." (*GMA* 17) But the transcendent supremacy of this "canon within the canon" of MacDonald's *oeuvre* is not made on the basis of any literary merit, since Lewis has already precluded any serious consideration of MacDonald as a literary artist. According to Lewis, MacDonald's artistic achievement is not a literary one at all, but rather belongs to what Lewis calls mythopoeic fantasy. Lewis hesitates to discuss the latter in strictly literary terms since,

---

[26] *GMA* 14; emphasis added. On this point Adelheid Kegler comments: "Lewis klassifiziert MacDonald als guten Mythopoeten, jedoch eher mittelmässigen Schriftsteller ... Leider wird dieser Klassifizierung in der MacDonald-Literatur häufig noch unhinterfragt übernommen" ["Lewis classifies MacDonald as a good creator of myth, but as a rather average writer ... Unfortunately this classification is often taken on uncritically in writing on MacDonald]. See "Einhundert Lichtjahre in neunzehn Stunden: Das rätselhafte Raumschiff in David Lindsay's *A Voyage to Arcturus*", *Inklings-Jahrbuch* 21 (2003), p. 162n4.

as myth, it is for Lewis in principle independent of language: "Myth does not essentially exist in *words* at all. We all agree that the story of Balder is a great myth, a thing of inexhaustible value. But whose version – whose *words* – are we thinking when we say this?" (*GMA* 15) As evidence of this claim, Lewis offers the anecdote of his hearing the story of Kafka's *The Castle* related in conversation and afterwards reading the book for himself. He claims, incredibly enough for those who find the quality of Kafka's prose disturbing, that "the reading added nothing." (*GMA* 16)

The date of publication of Lewis's *MacDonald Anthology* (1946) suggests that here Lewis was not consciously going against the Spirit of the Age and the mid-twentieth century "linguistic turn", although he was quite capable of (and indeed, one suspects, would rather have relished) such deliberate provocation.[27] Lewis's view, as he put it twenty-five years after the *MacDonald Anthology* in *An Experiment in Criticism* (1961), that Myth has a power and value "independent of its embodiment in any literary work"[28] may have a certain immediate plausibility, but it runs counter to the prevailing intellectual climate of the latter half of the twentieth century, which might be summed up in the slogan deriving from Derrida's *On Grammatology*: "*Il n'y a pas de hors-texte*" ["there is nothing outside of the text"].[29] More concretely, current debates about the success (or otherwise) of the translation of *The Lord of the Rings*, *The Lion, the Witch and the Wardrobe* and most recently *Northern Lights/The Golden Compass* into film versions would seem to raise questions about Lewis's assertion of the myth's in-principle independence of its literary form. It is also noteworthy how critics in areas other than literature (Lewis's examples are mime and film) tend to describe their particular medium in quasi-linguistic terms.[30] I suspect I am not alone in finding it hard to accept Lewis's claim that "the meaning, the suggestion, the

---

[27] See Lewis's inaugural lecture "De Descriptione Temporum" at Cambridge University where he presented himself as "Old Western Man", in *Selected Literary Essays* (ed W. Hooper) (Cambridge: Cambridge University Press, 1969); see also Gray, *Lewis* p. 2.

[28] C.S. Lewis, *An Experiment in Criticism* (Cambridge: Cambridge University Press, 1961), p. 41. It is interesting to note that Pullman is in explicit agreement with Lewis on this idea that "a myth is a story whose power is independent of its telling"; see Pullman's "A word or two about myths" in *The Myths Boxset* (Edinburgh: Canongate, 2005).

[29] Jacques Derrida, *Of Grammatology* (trans. Gayatri Spivak) (Baltimore: John Hopkins University Press, 1975), p. 158.

[30] See, for example, James Monaco, *How to read a film: language, history, theory* (3rd ed.) (Oxford: Oxford University Press, 2000).

radiance" that is "incarnate" in MacDonald's great works (*GMA* 17) is merely "a particular pattern of events which would equally delight and nourish if it had reached me by some medium which involved no words at all." (*GMA* 15) Indeed, in his edition of MacDonald's *Complete Fairy Tales*, U.C. Knoepflmacher has specifically blamed Lewis's influence (particularly through the latter's *MacDonald Anthology*) for the lack of critical attention to what he calls "the rhetorical sophistication of [MacDonald's] best work", so that:

> MacDonald's profoundly experimental and inter-textual fairy tales and fantasies, his subversive incursions into so many different nineteenth-century literary forms, and his delight in the friction and contradictions he could produce through his generic criss-crossings, went unnoticed.[31]

One example of MacDonald's stylistic virtuosity might be the fourth sentence of "The Wise Woman" which takes over 400 words to lead up to the bare fact that "something happened" (*CFT* 225-6). This might even be seen as a kind of prescient ironic commentary on Lewis's claim that what matters is the "events" which need no words at all, so that "[i]f the story is anywhere embodied in words, that is almost an accident" (*GMA* 15). Lewis's doubtful theory of language thus allows him to celebrate MacDonald's acts of myth-making genius, despite the latter's alleged shortcomings as a writer. Such damnation with faint praise—when Lewis separates the power of a myth from the limitations of its actual literary expression—is precisely one of the ways in which Lewis arguably "misreads" MacDonald. Whatever reservations one might have about MacDonald's "realist" fiction, for the most part his fantasy fiction is written in very interesting ways. And this is not simply a case of style (or indeed formal experimentation) for its own sake. The *content* of, for example, *The Light Princess*—interestingly a work omitted from Lewis's "canon within the MacDonald canon"—is literally inseparable from its literary *form*. In the meaning of this tale, the *tone* of its narration is crucial: levity is what it is all about.

However, Lewis not only attacks MacDonald's potency as a writer, whilst all the while praising him a spiritual master who through his mythopoeic genius baptised Lewis's imagination[32]; he also misreads the theological *content* of MacDonald's work. This is particularly relevant to a

---

[31] U.C. Knoepflmacher (ed.) *George MacDonald: The Complete Fairy Tales* (Harmondsworth: Penguin, 1999), pp. viii-ix. Hereafter cited in parentheses as *CFT*.

[32] *GMA* 21; see also C.S. Lewis, *Surprised by Joy* (London: Fontana, 1959), p. 146.

comparison of Pullman and MacDonald since the theology of C.S. Lewis to which Pullman objects is not necessarily to be identified with MacDonald's, despite the fact that Lewis has co-opted the latter. In her essay "George MacDonald and C.S. Lewis" in William Raeper's *The Gold Thread*, Catherine Durie shows how Lewis systematically misread MacDonald's theology. One important aspect of MacDonald's theology that Lewis "quietly drops" is what Durie calls "the childlikeness of God", and its corollary that: "MacDonald consistently claims that theology misrepresents God when it portrays him as the great king."[33] MacDonald's view of God is, says Durie, "a long way from the hierarchical and authoritative images that move Lewis".[34] Lewis's misreadings of MacDonald culminate in *The Great Divorce* when he makes the *character* "George MacDonald" express views directly opposite to views the real MacDonald actually held. As Durie puts it:

> Lewis and MacDonald are here made to change places; but the MacDonald who makes such forceful points is a ventriloquist's dummy. It is Lewis's voice which subverts the real MacDonald's belief in hell as a temporary purifying force, and heaven as the home of every one of God's children.[35]

These misreadings of MacDonald by Lewis bear directly on issues that Pullman has raised in relation to Lewis. Firstly, Pullman's idea of "the republic of heaven" depends precisely on his opposition to the idea of God as king (an opposition which MacDonald shared, but Lewis edited out). Secondly, on the issue of universal salvation, Lewis actively misrepresents MacDonald and makes him reject the idea of universalism that MacDonald actually espoused, and according to which not only the mildly rebellious Susan, but also the seriously rebellious Satan (or "Samoil", as he appears in *Lilith*[36]), will ultimately be saved.[37] So even if Lewis does let Susan be damned (in both senses of "let"), then MacDonald certainly wouldn't. This raises the possibility that Pullman may have more in common with

---

[33] William Raeper (ed.), *The Gold Thread: Essays on George MacDonald* (Edinburgh: Edinburgh University Press, 1990), p. 173.

[34] Ibid.

[35] Ibid., p.175.

[36] See George MacDonald, *Lilith* (Grand Rapids: Eerdmans, 1981), p. 107, where "Samoil" (probably to be identified with "Sammael") is the name of the Shadow. 'Sammael' is also related to the Satanic figure of "Zamiel" who appears in Pullman's *Count Karlstein or The Ride of the Demon Huntsman* (London: Corgi Yearling, 1998), and is derived from Carl Maria von Weber's opera *Der Freischütz*.

[37] George MacDonald, *Lilith* (Grand Rapids: Eerdmans, 1981), pp. 217-8.

MacDonald than we would expect if we assumed that MacDonald and Lewis shared identical (and to Pullman offensive) theological views.

MacDonald and Pullman

What then could MacDonald and Pullman be seen to have in common? First of all, *a faith in stories*, and more specifically, stories that appeal to what MacDonald called "the fantastic imagination" (I put it this way partly to circumvent Pullman's avowed dislike of the genre "fantasy literature"). Stories, and more specifically fairy stories, are a way of communicating in a non-conceptual way; for MacDonald it is a kind of category mistake to expect a fairy tale "to impart anything defined, anything notionally recognizable" (*CFT* 8). MacDonald's view of language not only echoes (especially German) Romanticism; it also seems to prefigure Kristeva's distinction between "the symbolic" and "the semiotic" (or the "phenotext" and the "genotext")[38], when he replies to the claim that words—unlike music—"are meant and fitted to carry a precise meaning":

> It is very seldom indeed that they carry the exact meaning of any user of them! And if they can be so used as to convey definite meaning, it does not follow that they ought never to carry anything else… They can convey a scientific fact, or throw a shadow of her child's dream on the heart of a mother. (*CFT* 8)

This idea that "Sometimes fairy stories may best say what's to be said" is of course particularly associated with Lewis[39], but he certainly didn't invent it; it was the common property of other Inklings such as Tolkien and Barfield and derives ultimately from Romanticism, and especially perhaps German Romanticism. Lewis's version of the concrete imaginative experience of myth versus the abstract intellectual understanding of allegory has tended to be set up in a way that resonates with the New Critical privileging of the organic unity of a non-conceptual, non-paraphrasable transcendental meaning.[40] This derives principally from Coleridge, with the emphasis on the organic unity of meaning; but there is

---

[38] See Julia Kristeva, *Revolution in Poetic Language* (trans. Margaret Waller) (New York: Columbia University Press, 1984); extracts in *The Kristeva Reader* (ed Toril Moi) (Oxford: Blackwell, 1986). On MacDonald and Kristeva, see Chapter One above, "George MacDonald, Julia Kristeva and the Black Sun".

[39] See C.S. Lewis, *On This and Other Worlds* (= U.S. *On Stories and Other Essays on Literature*) (ed. W. Hooper) (London: Collins, 1982; also Collins Fount, 1984).

[40] See Gray, *Lewis*, p. 33.

also a different kind of Romanticism which stresses, if not the indeterminacy of meaning, then at least the diversity of meaning as received differently by different hearers. I use "hearers" advisedly because in MacDonald's essay "The Fantastic Imagination" the key example for how art communicates is *music* or in this case specifically the sonata. (*CFT* 8-9) As MacDonald puts it: "The greatest forces lie in the region of the uncomprehended." (*CFT* 9)

Taking music as the condition to which all the arts aspire was central to German Romanticism (whence the later European Symbolist movement took the idea[41]). Pullman too has related his writing to musical experience. In the powerful final sequence of *Northern Lights*, when Lyra (and indeed the reader) are moving into "the region of the uncomprehended" as Lyra advances into another world, Pullman explicitly echoes a line from the German symbolist poet Stefan George's poem "*Entrückung* [Rapture]": "*Ich fühle luft von anderen planeten* [I feel air from other planets]" when Lord Asriel cries: "Can you feel that wind? A wind from another world!"[42] Pullman has intertextually related the effect of this transition into another world to Schoenberg's setting of George's poem "*Entrückung*" in his String Quartet No. 2, when the music leaves the world of tonality altogether and moves into the strange new world of atonality[43]. Here, in an archetypally Romantic gesture, literary Symbolism (George's poem) fuses with music (Schoenberg's Quartet) and illuminates the strange power of this numinous moment in Pullman's novel which stretches towards a kind of *mysterium tremendum et fascinans,* as Rudolf Otto famously described the experience of "The Holy".[44] Lyra's first full experience of the Aurora or "Northern Lights" had moved her to tears with a vision which "was so beautiful it was almost holy" (*NL* 183), though perhaps we might have expected the rhetoric of "the sublime" rather than 'the beautiful" for a sight whose "immensity … was scarcely conceivable" (*NL* 183). The Romantic register returns at the climax of the novel when the Aurora is described, for example, as "a cataract of glory" (*NL* 392). This rhetoric of the sublime and the numinous seems to echo the claim of MacDonald—

---

[41] See for example Marcel Raymond, *From Baudelaire to Surrealism* (London: Methuen, 1970).

[42] Pullman, Philip, *Northern Lights* (= U.S. *The Golden Compass*) (London: Scholastic, 1995), p. 394. Hereafter cited in parentheses as *NL*.

[43] See child_lit LISTERV (July 27, 2000). Also cited in Millicent Lenz with Carole Scott (eds), *His Dark Materials Illuminated* (Detroit: Wayne State UP, 2005) pp. 5-6.

[44] Rudolf Otto, *The Idea of the Holy* (trans. J. W. Harvey) (2nd ed.) (Oxford: Oxford University Press, 1950).

whose supreme gift according to Lewis was to mediate "Holiness"[45]—that it was supremely in music and (in the widest sense) the fairy tale, those products of "the fantastic imagination", that we encounter those "greatest forces [that] lie in the region of the uncomprehended" (*CFT* 9).

Such attunement to the diverse possibilities of interpretation—Lyra relates her numinous experience of the Aurora to her trance-like state while consulting the alethiometer (*NL* 183)—is foregrounded by MacDonald in his essay "The Fantastic Imagination"; it is characteristic not only of German Romanticism but also of postmodernism. Both Pullman and MacDonald have been linked with both these "movements" (or climates of thought and sensibility). Pullman's qualified alignment with postmodernism was noted above. Various critics have claimed that MacDonald in some ways anticipated postmodernism.[46] This should not be a surprise, given Andrew Bowie's contention that in certain crucial respects German Romanticism anticipated postmodernism by well over a century. [47] The considerable debt of MacDonald to specifically *German* Romanticism is well known; we need look no further than the epigraphs to *Phantastes*, and especially those by Novalis. Philip Pullman too has in personal correspondence been willing to "cheerfully own up" to a nostalgia for German Romanticism.[48] For example, the list of "Works consulted and ideas stolen from" at the end of Pullman's *Count Karlstein or The Ride of the Deman Huntsman* includes "Caspar David Friedrich, *various pictures*" as well as Carl Maria von Weber's archetypal Romantic opera *Der Freischütz*, from which the plot of *Count Karlstein* is largely derived. *Count Karlstein* as well as *Clockwork* simply exudes German Romanticism in general and E.T.A. Hoffmann in particular. Similar MacDonald tales would be "The Cruel Painter" and the tale of another Prague student, Cosmo von Wehrstahl, located at the centre of *Phantastes*.

---

[45] Lewis, *Surprised by Joy*, p. 145.

[46] On MacDonald and postmodernism see Roderick McGillis (ed.) *The Princess and the Goblin* and *The Princess and Curdie* (Oxford: Oxford University Press, 1990), pp. xvi-xxviii; Stephen Prickett in William Raeper (ed.) *The Gold Thread* (Edinburgh: Edinburgh University Press, 1990), pp. 123-4; and Deborah Thacker and Jean Webb, *Introducing Children's Literature : from Romanticism to Postmodernism* (London: Routledge, 2002) pp. 42-4; 140-2.

[47] See Andrew Bowie, *Aesthetics and Subjectivity: From Kant to Nietzsche* (2nd ed.) (Manchester: Manchester University Press, 2003), pp. 8-15.

[48] Letter of 26 June 2005. In a subsequent letter of 5 April 2008 he claims to have been reading Hoffmann "for most of [his] adult life", and to have read Novalis's *Heinrich von Ofterdingen* 25 years ago, though since it's fifteen years since he began writing *His Dark Materials*, "there may well be some influence there".

The debt of both MacDonald and Pullman to *English* Romanticism is also evident. MacDonald was deeply interested in Wordsworth, Coleridge and Shelley, as well as in Blake (though the extent of his knowledge of Blake is unclear). Pullman of course has declared himself of Blake's party, though the general Romantic attempt to re-imagine religious experience in a non-dogmatic and non-supernatural way clearly informs his work, as it also does that of MacDonald.[49] Pullman has declared the importance to him of his traditional Anglican background; however, his evident love of Milton and Blake align him with the tradition of English dissent. MacDonald also came from a tradition of dissent, though the Congregationalist tradition to which he belonged tended to be dominated by Calvinist theology, with its "puritanical martinet of a God".[50] MacDonald not only aligned himself with the Christian Platonist tradition going back to Plotinus and Origen (also a universalist); he was also willing to explore the current of Gnosticism implicit in it.[51] That tradition included Boehme and Novalis, as well as more exotic writers such as Swedenborg, whom Blake memorably, if ambivalently, dismissed in *The Marriage of Heaven Hell*. MacDonald's predilection for the Wise Woman or Great-great-grandmother motif has also been widely seen as connected with the Sophia figure in Gnosticism.[52].

Pullman too admits to an interest in Gnosticism, citing as a source Harold Bloom's novel *The Flight to Lucifer: a Gnostic Fantasy*, and raising the question of Gnosticism in his dialogue with Rowan Williams.[53] But even if the oracle himself had not announced it, the Gnostic influence in *His Dark Materials* would have been clearly evident. Pullman's so-called atheism could be seen as a Gnostic anti-theology in which, like some early Gnostics, he re-tells the Genesis story backwards; in this counter-version, the Fall is really an advance in human potential enabled by good offices of the serpent, the bringer of wisdom, who succeeds in

---

[49] See for example M. H. Abrams, *Natural supernaturalism: Tradition and Revolution in Romantic Literature* (New York: Norton, 1973). I have developed this theme in my book *Fantasy, Myth and the Measure of Truth: Tales of Pullman, Lewis, Tolkien, MacDonald and Hoffmann* (Palgrave Macmillan, 2008), especially in the Prelude, "Pullman's 'High Argument'".

[50] William Raeper, *George MacDonald* (Tring: Lion, 1987), p. 242.

[51] Ibid., pp. 240; 243; 257-8.

[52] See for example Deidre Hayward, "The Mystical Sophia: More on the Great Grandmother in the Princess Books", *North Wind: Journal of George MacDonald Studies*, 13, 1994.

[53] Lyn Haill (ed.), *Darkness Illuminated* (London: National Theatre / Oberon Books, 2004), p. 87.

circumventing the usurped power of the demiurge who is not the true God at all but merely the jealous creator of a shameful and imprisoning world.[54] The anti-clerical, anti-hierarchical and in some cases anti-patriarchal elements that inform historical Gnosticism reappear in Pullman's work. Above all, there seems to have been in historical Gnosticism a commitment to the power of stories narrating spiritual experience: "Every one of them generates something new every day ... for no-one is considered initiated [or: 'mature'] among them unless he develops some enormous fictions", complained St Irenaeus.[55] The development of "enormous fictions" intended to mediate spiritual insight could certainly be seen as characteristic of both Pullman and MacDonald. Both *Lilith* and *His Dark Materials* are by any reckoning enormous in scope, comparable, *mutatis mutandis*, with David Lindsay's *Voyage to Arcturus* or perhaps Goethe's *Faust*—MacDonald himself apparently nursed the ambition to see *Lilith* compared to a kind of modern *Divine Comedy*.[56] Lewis's "Space Trilogy" also seems to belong in this family constellation. Whether, or how, Lewis's other work might fit into this family group is a matter for discussion. Presumably Pullman would disavow Lewis, but as I have argued above, a bit of internecine Oedipal conflict or misreading *à la* Bloom is only to be expected. And as I have suggested elsewhere[57], Lewis's Christian Platonism comes much closer to Gnosticism (especially in the "Space Trilogy"[58]) than one might expect, given the appropriation of his work by the orthodox. In this too, Lewis seems actually closer to the spirit of MacDonald than even his own more orthodox pronouncements might suggest.

---

[54] This summary of some key motifs in Gnosticism is dependent on, *inter alia*: Hans Jonas, *The Gnostic Religion: The Message of the Alien God and the Beginnings of Christianity* (2nd rev. ed.) (Boston: Beacon Press, 1963); James M. Robinson (ed.) *The Nag Hammadi Library in English* (Leiden: Brill, 1977); Elaine Pagels, *The Gnostic Gospels* (Harmondsworth: Penguin, 1981); Kurt Rudolph, *Gnosis: The Nature and History of Gnosticism* (Edinburgh: T. and T. Clark, 1983); Bentley Layton (ed.) *The Gnostic Scriptures: A New Translation with Annotations and Introductions* (London : SCM, 1987); Giovanni Filoramo, *A History of Gnosticism* (Oxford: Blackwell, 1990); A.H.B. Logan, *The Gnostics: Identifying an Ancient Christian Cult* (Edinburgh: T. and T. Clark, 2006).

[55] Cited by Pagels, *The Gnostic Gospels*, p. 48.

[56] Raeper, *George MacDonald*, pp. 367-9.

[57] Gray, *Lewis*, pp. 45-6.

[58] Which Pullman "read avidly" as a boy in his clergyman grandfather's study, though he "can't take them at all now" (personal correspondence, 5 April 2008).

Postscript

Who George MacDonald "misreads", and who his literary father-figure might be, is another question. At the beginning of *Phantastes*, Anodos's fairy grandmother is dismissive of his knowledge of his male precursors, and chides his ignorance of his female relatives; great-grandmothers and sisters are more to the point.[59] The great-grandmother/Wise Woman motif is a marked feature of MacDonald's work, and can be interpreted as indicating MacDonald's interest in *pre-oedipal* maternal material (as I have argued in an essay offering Kristevan reading of *Phantastes*[60]). Whether MacDonald's reliance on Novalis and the Sophia myth may suggest a different scenario than Bloom's aggressively Oedipal one, and whether this may allow a way to circumvent the Eve versus Lilith double-bind, predicated on what Gilbert and Gubar call, following Virginia Woolf, "Milton's bogey"[61] remains, I think, an open question. Behind the double misreading of Lewis by Pullman, and MacDonald by Lewis, there might be a link between MacDonald's and Pullman's attempts to get beyond the power nexus of patriarchal binary thinking. Such a link would have much to do with the subterranean connections of Romanticism and postmodernism, with both of which "movements' (or "styles" or "structures of sensibility") both MacDonald and Pullman have been associated.

---

[59] George MacDonald, *Phantastes: A Faërie Romance for Men and Women* (London: Dent/Everyman, 1915), p. 5.
[60] See Chapter One above, "George MacDonald, Julia Kristeva and the Black Sun.".
[61] Gilbert and Gubar, *The Madwoman in the Attic*, pp. 187-95.

CHAPTER NINE

WITCHES' TIME IN PHILIP PULLMAN, C.S. LEWIS AND GEORGE MACDONALD

Every seven years, scientists tell us, our body entirely transforms itself. Thus although, as we shall see, Princess Irene's Great-great-grandmother would disagree[1], the author of the present paper is literally not the same person who came to Roehampton seven years ago to give a paper at a Religious Studies conference.[2] That paper was on a topic in philosophy, and looked at an (I hoped) impressive array of continental philosophers including Gadamer, Derrida, Heidegger and Nietzsche—all of whom, as it happens, had quite a bit to say about "Time". Seven years later, the papers I give tend to be on what might be called "Fantasy Fiction for Children of All Ages", by the likes of George MacDonald and Philip Pullman. This does not mean, however, that I have lost interest in philosophy. On the contrary, one of the things that draws me to the writings of MacDonald, Pullman and similar writers is the fact that they are raising, it seems to me, some big philosophical questions in the context of Children's Literature. As Pullman has said in another context, Children's Literature is perhaps one of the few places you *can* raise big questions these days[3]—in contrast,

---

[1] For her, "Shapes are only dresses … That which is inside is the same all the time." See George MacDonald, *The Princess and the Goblin* and *The Princess and Curdie* (ed. Rod McGillis) (Oxford: OUP World's Classics, 1990), p. 209. Hereafter cited in parentheses as *PGPC*. I return to this passage in conclusion.

[2] My decision not to rework this conference paper so as to eliminate all traces of its original context is influenced by Gadamer's defence of the hermeneutical relevance of the "occasionality" of a piece of work. See Hans-Georg Gadamer, *Truth and Method* (trans. Weinsheimer & Marshall) (new ed.) (New York: Continuum, 2004), pp. 138-41. The invitation from the organizers of the 2006 Roehampton conference on "Time Everlasting: Representations of Past, Present and Future in Children's Literature" was to share ideas informally rather than to deliver a formal paper.

[3] According to Pullman in his Carnegie Medal Acceptance Speech: "There are some themes, some subjects, too large for adult fiction; they can only be dealt with adequately in a children's book."

ironically, to a university Philosophy department. Or so I am informed by my son, a recent graduate in Philosophy at one of Britain's most prestigious universities. On the award of his degree, I thought it safe to send him a copy of Philip Pullman's *I Was a Rat!* He loved all those wonderful passages about "the Royal Metaphysician". More seriously, it has often been pointed out that Pullman and MacDonald have in common a determination to take their child readers seriously; they are willing to trust in the capacity of children to make what they can of supposedly "difficult" ideas.[4]

The bottom line is that children too are existing individuals, in an existentialist sense. They surely have, or soon will have, an at least tacit knowledge that they too are mortal, subject to time—a vertiginous sense of simply finding themselves in the world, and only temporarily. There must be many studies which blend the insights of developmental psychology and existentialist philosophy in their exploration of what might be called the negative "Aha-moment", what Heidegger calls the experience of "Angst" or a "brush with Being"—that appalling moment which we have all had when we first realize that death is not something that just happens to other people, whether in books, or films or in real life.[5] Actually it happens to yours truly, and sooner than seems conceivable. What Philip Larkin describes in his poem "Aubade" may become a more frequent, if no less unwelcome, visitor, as we grow older. But there is always a first time to encounter "our death", as Pullman puts it in *The Amber Spyglass*, and we don't have to be adult to have this particular visitor, though we may grow up pretty quickly. As is sometimes said in another context, how was it for you?

I have to confess that genesis of the present paper lies not so much in careful, methodological reflection on the nature of "Time", as in the moment when one particular passage in Pullman's *Northern Lights* suddenly leapt to mind. This is the conversation between Lyra and the witch Serafina Pekkala that begins when Lyra asks her: "How long do

---

See http://www.randomhouse.com/features/pullman/author/carnegie.html

[4] See for example Shelley King, "'Without Lyra we would understand neither the New nor the Old Testament': Exegesis, Allegory and Reading *The Golden Compass*", in Millicent Lenz with Carole Scott (eds), *His Dark Materials Illuminated* (Detroit: Wayne State University Press, 2005), pp. 109-11.

[5] See for example M.W. Speece and S.B. Brent, "Children's Understanding of Death", *Journal of Child Development* Vol.55, 1984, pp. 1671-1686; A. Dyregrov, *Grief in Children* (London: Jessica Kingsley, 2007). References kindly supplied by Lorna Gray who is researching "the Management of Death and Loss in the Primary School" at the University of Chichester.

witches live?"[6] Up to a thousand years, replies Serafina, though she herself is a mere three hundred or so. Then she continues, and her opening words echo almost verbatim the response of Irene's great-great grandmother in *The Princess and the Goblin* when the princess says she doesn't understand: "I daresay not. I didn't expect you would. But that's no reason why I shouldn't say it … I will explain it all when you are older…" (*PGPC* 14) Similarly, Serafina says:

> "You are too young, Lyra, too young to understand this, but I shall tell you any way and you'll understand it later; men pass in front of our eyes like butterflies, creatures of a brief season. We love them; they are brave, proud, beautiful, clever; and they die almost at once. We bear their children, who are witches if they are female, human if not; and then in the blink of an eye they are gone, felled, slain, lost. Our sons, too. When a little boy is growing, he thinks he is immortal. His mother knows he isn't. Each time becomes more painful, until finally your heart is broken. Perhaps that is when Yambe-Akka comes for you. She is older than the tundra. Perhaps, for her, witches' lives are as brief as men's are to us." (*NL* 314)

There is certainly a suggestion here that time is relative; and perhaps even a suggestion that time is gendered. Although the distinction is made between witches and human beings, the way it is set up means that for the most part Serafina is talking specifically about *men* and not about human beings in general. So there is at least the possibility that "women's time" (to use Julia Kristeva's phrase[7]) may be different from *both* witches' time *and* men's time. Whether women's time might be more like the former than the latter is, I think, an interesting question.

Be that as it may, Pullman is in this passage introducing to younger readers the immemorial themes of *tempus fugit* [time flies] and *memento mori* [remember you too must die], more brutally expressed in Pozzo's furious cry in *Waiting for Godot*:

> "Have you not done tormenting me with your accursed time! It's abominable! … [O]ne day we were born, one day we shall die, the same day, the same second, is that not enough for you? *(Calmer.)* They give birth astride of a grave, the light gleams an instant, then it's night once more."[8]

---

[6] Pullman, Philip, *Northern Lights* (= U.S. *The Golden Compass*) (London: Scholastic, 1995), p. 314. Hereafter cited in parentheses as *NL*.

[7] Julia Kristeva, "Women's Time" in *The Kristeva Reader* (ed Toril Moi) (Oxford: Blackwell, 1986).

[8] Samuel Beckett, *Waiting for Godot* (London: Faber and Faber, 1965), p. 89.

Like Beckett, Pullman is telling all the truth of what used to be called "the human condition", but he is telling it slant (to use Emily Dickinson's phrase)[9]. He speaks of human subjection to time and death indirectly, or circuitously (to echo Dickinson again[10]), mediated through the experience of the witch Serafina Pekkala. Younger readers are not *directly* confronted with the brevity of life and inevitability of death; but the inference is there, if they are ready to make it.

This passage is also about love as well as death. It introduces the theme of the effect of time on physical love—not a theme likely to seem immediately relevant or interesting to younger readers. The ageless Serafina Pekkala is reluctant to visit the by now very old Farder Coram lest he is made to feel the shame of age—"he would be ashamed of his own age, and I wouldn't want to make him feel that." (*NL* 315) By thus displacing onto the infinitely glamorous witch a concern probably remote to most young people, Pullman can introduce an awareness of the problems of aging. Ironically, while it is the traditional witch who above all expresses the feelings of horror and disgust induced by the aging process, Pullman uses his highly nubile witch to suggest a more sensitive and compassionate perspective on the real emotional and psychological problems caused by the effects of time.

As already mentioned, Pullman introduces head-on the figure of death in the third of the *His Dark Materials* trilogy, *The Amber Spyglass*. In the chapter entitled "Lyra and her Death", set in the "suburbs of the dead", Lyra and her companions seek their way to the world of the dead to find Lyra's friend Roger. Here they encounter "the deaths" of those who by chance or accident have found themselves living (so to speak) in "the holding area" of the world of the dead. These inhabitants of the suburbs of the dead are shocked that Lyra and her companions are not accompanied by their "deaths", the literal embodiment of each individual's death that is constantly with them. As one of them tells Lyra:

> "We had 'em all the time and we never knew. See, everyone has a death. It goes everywhere with 'em, all their life long, right close by … the moment you're born, your death comes into the world with you, and it's your death that takes you out."[11]

Besides echoing folk traditions the world over (most strongly perhaps the

---

[9] Emily Dickinson, *The Complete Poems* (ed Thomas H. Johnson) (London: Faber and Faber, 1975), no. 1129, "Tell all the Truth but tell it slant", pp. 506-7.
[10] Ibid.
[11] Philip Pullman, *The Amber Spyglass* (London: Scholastic, 2000), p. 275. Hereafter cited in parentheses as *AS*.

Mexican "Day of the Dead"), Pullman's figures of death seem to embody what Heidegger called the "mineness [*Jemeinigkeit*]" of my death[12]; it's the only thing that is ultimately only mine. Significantly, Pullman writes "death" without a capital letter. It's not an abstraction, not something remote or general, but infinitely close, intimate and banal, like the skeletal old death lying in bed with Granny and pinching her cheek (*AS* 278). In what might be interpreted as a mythological representation of Heidegger's concept of "Being-unto-death [*Sein-zum-Tode*]", Granny's death says: "That's the answer, that's it, that's what you've got to do, say welcome, make friends, be kind, invite your deaths to come close to you ..." (*AS* 279)

Heidegger's *Being and Time* was famously used by Rudolf Bultmann as a basis for demythologizing the New Testament[13], and also, and perhaps more relevantly to Pullman, by Hans Jonas to demythologize the Gnostic scriptures[14]. Pullman might even be seen as *re-mythologizing* a range of existentialist ideas. The chapter "Lyra and her death" could be seen as a mythologization not only of Heidegger's "Being-unto-death", but also of the traditional theme of the *ars moriendi* [the art of dying], but without the Christian consolations. This question of the Christian consolations will come to the fore when we turn to C.S. Lewis's treatment of time and mortality, and Pullman's rather strident criticisms of Lewis. For the moment, it is important to note that Pullman not only has an implicit (or mythologized) *thanatology*, but also an explicit *eschatology*, or teaching on the End. Again, this will come more sharply into focus when we look at Pullman's criticisms of Lewis, but it is worth indicating here the kind of quasi-Wordsworthian mystical pantheism suggested later in *The Amber Spyglass* when Lyra tells one of the ghosts in the world of the dead:

> "But your daemons en't just *nothing* now; they're part of everything. All the atoms that were them, they've gone into the air and the wind and the trees and the earth and all the living things. They'll never vanish. They're just part of everything. And that's exactly what'll happen to you ..." (*AS* 335)

Another ghost takes up Lyra's theme: "[W]e'll be alive again in a thousand blades of grass, and a million leaves, we'll be falling in the raindrops and blowing in the fresh breeze, we'll be glittering in the dew

---

[12] Martin Heidegger, *Being and Time* (trans. John Macquarrie and Edward Robinson) (New York: Harper, 1962), p. 284.

[13] Rudolf Bultmann, *New Testament and Mythology and Other Basic Writings* (ed & trans. by Schubert M. Ogden) (Augsburg: Fortress, 1984).

[14] Hans Jonas, *The Gnostic Religion* (2nd rev. ed.) (Boston: Beacon Press, 1963).

under the stars and the moon …" (*AS* 336) And when the ghost of Lyra's old friend Roger becomes the first to achieve release from the world of the dead, it is presented as a moment of intoxication:

> He took a step forward, and turned to look back at Lyra, and laughed in surprise as he found himself turning into the night, the starlight, the air … and then he was gone, leaving behind such a vivid little burst of happiness that Will was reminded of the bubbles in a glass of champagne. (*AS* 382)

Elsewhere I have—perhaps ungenerously—called this Pullman's "Happy Hour" version of pantheistic mystical surrender.[15]

Given this sunny view of extinction, it is perhaps a little ironical that Pullman should accuse Lewis of taking death too lightly, as when he criticises Lewis for his allegedly "horrible" message that being killed in a train crash is the best thing ever if you end up in Heaven.[16] I think that Pullman might be accused of quoting Lewis rather out of context. One can see that portraying the *eschaton* (or the End of Time) as "that great school hols in the sky" has its limitations—if also, to be honest, its attractiveness, not only to children but also to those of us in the teaching profession! I have written elsewhere about Lewis's sense of what I called the truant frivolity characteristic of the Joy that is "the serious business of heaven".[17] And Lewis does take death very seriously, above all of course in *A Grief Observed*, but also in *The Chronicles of Narnia*, and especially in *The Magician's Nephew*.[18] A central theme of the latter book is how Digory deals with the fact that his mother is dying. It is of course also about how young Jack Lewis dealt with the fact that *his* mother was dying in Belfast at pretty well the same time that Digory's mother was dying in London (Lewis is very precise in specifying the temporal location of *The Magician's Nephew*). There is in the latter a re-enactment of the temptation scene in Eden—re-enactments of Eden figure largely in books by both of those great Miltonians, Lewis and Pullman. Jadis, the White Witch in waiting, tempts Digory to eat of the silver apple of life, and

---

[15] See "Pullman, Lewis, MacDonald and the anxiety of influence" above.

[16] Pullman interview with Susan Roberts for Christian Aid, November 2002 [http://www.surefish.co.uk/culture/features/pullman_interview.htm] quoted in Hugh Rayment-Pickard, *The Devil's Account: Philip Pullman and Christianity* (London: Darton Longman and Todd, 2004)), p.45.

[17] William Gray, *C.S. Lewis* (Plymouth: Northcote House, 1998), p. 98, quoting C.S. Lewis, *Letters to Malcolm: Chiefly on Prayer* (London: Geoffrey Bles, 1964; Collins Fount, 1977), p. 95; see also C.S. Lewis, *Selected Books* (London: HarperCollins, 2002), p. 283.

[18] See Chapter Five above, "Death, Myth and Reality in C.S. Lewis".

acquire eternal life. She has already done so, and, we later learn, "has won her heart's desire. She has unwearying strength like a goddess. But length of days with an evil heart is only length of misery and already she begins to know it."[19] While Pullman's witches have a natural longevity that brings into sharp relief the brevity of human life, Lewis's witch has acquired an immunity to the passing of time which is unnatural (or to be more precise, *sinful*, since it depends on a kind of repetition of the Original Sin). When Digory is tempted by the witch to eat of the apple and live forever, he gives a bluff reply redolent of Lewis's "mere Christianity": "No thanks ... I don't know that I care much about living on and on after everyone I know is dead. I'd rather live an ordinary time and die and go to Heaven." (*MN* 150) Good, ordinary Christianity is enough for a chap like Digory, who has a kind of understated heroism masquerading as mere decency, typical of Lewis as well as post-war Britain. There is also perhaps the suggestion of a kind of disgust at the self-obsession which Lewis saw as inherent in the occult dabblings of decadent late Romantics such as Yeats. Jadis and also Uncle Andrew are pilloried throughout the book for their egotistical insistence that (in George MacDonald's terms) they are "Somebody"[20] and therefore above the rules of ordinary mortals. Lewis has no time for the Romantic overreacher such as Lord Asriel. If, for some in the Romantic tradition, Satan may be a kind of hero, then Lewis is proposing a Christian anti-hero. For Lewis the Fall is no *felix culpa*, no blessing in disguise (it is not even in disguise, one suspects, for Pullman). Lewis's ordinariness is not natural, however, but comes from faith, resisting the temptation to think you are above the ordinary. Digory's faith really is tested when it is not the saving of his own life but that of his mother that is the reward for disobeying Aslan. What decides him in this "most terrible choice" is his glimpse of Jadis's essential meanness, when she appeals to Digory's selfishness by suggesting he leave Polly behind. Digory realises that "there might be things more terrible even than losing someone you love by death" (*MN* 163)—a hard enough lesson at any age, but especially for a child. Having learned the lesson, Digory is of course let off the hook, in that he is given another apple which does magically cure his mother. The young Jack Lewis had no such reprieve.

Given Lewis's ambivalent feelings about Romanticism, it is interesting to look at his first encounter with George MacDonald in this light. When

---

[19] C.S. Lewis, *The Magician's Nephew* [1955] (London: HarperCollins, 1996), p. 162. Hereafter cited in parentheses as *MN*.
[20] Like the Princess in "The Wise Woman, or the Lost Princess"; see U.C. Knoepflmacher (ed.), *George MacDonald: The Complete Fairy Tales* (Harmondsworth: Penguin, 1999), p. 226. Hereafter cited in parentheses as *CFT*.

he first read MacDonald's *Phantastes* in 1916 he was, he tells us, "waist deep in Romanticism", and likely, he says, "to flounder into its darker and more evil forms"[21]. Certainly *Phantastes* was "romantic enough", he says, but it felt different; and that difference was goodness, Lewis adds, though his teenage self would have been shocked had anyone suggested such a thing[22]. MacDonald's fairy tales are also centrally concerned with goodness, how we acquire it and how we lose it. Arguably, however, they are not in any obvious sense didactic, apart from "The Wise Woman", which is *about* teaching goodness.

There are certainly traditional wicked witches in MacDonald's fairy tales, from Princess Makemnoit in "The Light Princess", through the wicked swamp-fairy or witch in "Little Daylight", to Watho in "The History of Photogen and Nycteris". Apart from her initial cursing of the princess with a lack of gravity, the main wickedness of the witch Makemnoit lies in her draining of the lake. The evil machinations of the witches in "Little Daylight" and "The History of Photogen and Nycteris" have, however, more to do with the distortion of time. In both cases the natural—or maybe patriarchal?—order of day and night is reversed, so that both Nycteris and Princess Daylight only ever know the night, and have never seen the sun. Of course in the end "All is Well", as the last chapter of "The History of Photogen and Nycteris" is entitled, and the heroines of both stories finally see the light of day. For although the wicked witches may do their worst, in this case by reversing the order of day and night, it is "of no consequence", MacDonald insists in a kind of theodicy inserted into "Little Daylight", which echoes a major theme in *At the Back of the North Wind*: "[F]or what they do never succeeds; nay, in the end it brings about the very thing they are trying to prevent ... [F]or although from the beginning of the world they have really helped instead of thwarting the good fairies, not one of them is a bit wiser for it." (*CFT* 161)

As well as traditional wicked witches, however, there also in MacDonald's work what might be termed good witches. We meet the first of these grandmother figures with young eyes in the first chapter of *Phantastes*, where Anodos's shape-shifting grandmother changes size in order to illustrate to Anados the relativity of size or spatial extension. Such an insistence on the relativity of spatial dimensions also extends to the relativity of time. The eponymous wise woman in the "double tale" of "The Wise Woman, or the Lost Princess" shows the relativity of time and

---

[21] C.S. Lewis, *George MacDonald: An Anthology* (London: Geoffrey Bles, 1946), p. 20.
[22] Ibid., p. 21.

space as she manipulates them both in her work of bringing a range of characters ultimately to salvation. MacDonald is careful to distinguish the Wise Woman from the traditional witch, when he writes: "In some countries she would have been called a witch; but that would have been a mistake, for she never did any thing wicked, and had more power than any witch would have." (*CFT* 229) That the Wise Woman might be a so-called "white witch" is suggested when her black cloak gapes to reveal underneath a garment which is, says MacDonald, quoting Spenser's description of Una in *The Faerie Queene* (1.12:22):

> All lilly white, withoutten spot or pride,
> That seemed like silke and silver woven neare;
> But neither silke nor silver therein did appeare. (*CFT* 229)

This suggestion of the brilliant splendour hidden beneath the Wise Woman's cloak culminates in a kind of transfiguration scene at the end of the story when she is revealed (though only to one or two) in her full radiance.

The connection of the word "witch" with "wise" is a much-debated etymological point. If the Wise Woman is, it seems, more than a mere witch, for my present purposes I want to treat her as *at least* a kind of white witch, in order to explore her relation to time. Although she has great knowledge and powers, the Wise Woman's purpose is to lead people to the point where they themselves will voluntarily embrace the truth. At the beginning of the fourth chapter of "The Wise Woman", we are told that the Wise Woman "knew exactly what [the princess] was thinking; but it was one thing to understand the princess, and quite another to make the princess understand her: that would require time." (*CFT* 242) At the end of a long series of trials and tests, princess Rosamond finds herself before "a woman perfectly beautiful, neither old nor young; for hers was the old age of everlasting youth" (*CFT* 293). This mysterious women turns out to be the Wise Woman, who after this revelation dons again her long dark cloak. To Rosamond's question whether "it was you all the time?" the Wise Woman replies: "It always is me, all the time." (*CFT* 294) The dialogue continues:

> "But which is the real you?" asked Rosamond; "this or that?"
> "Or a thousand others?" returned the wise woman. "But the one you have just seen is the likest to the real me that you are able to see just yet — but—. And that me you could not have seen a little while ago.— But, my darling child," she went on … "you must not think, because you have seen me once, that therefore you are capable of seeing me at all times. No; there

are many things in you that must be changed before that can be." (*CFT* 294)

Overcome by shame, the princess asks the Wise Woman how she could have loved such a "hateful little wretch", to which the Wise Woman replies: "I saw, through it all, what you were going to be ... But remember you have yet only *begun* to be what I saw." (*CFT* 294) Evidently this (white) witch's time is different from the time that Rosamond, and the other characters, occupy. It also has a curious relation to what we might call authorial time. For all the insistence on the freedom of the characters in this story, there is also (for me anyway) an uncomfortable sense of authorial control. It seems that not only the Wise Woman, but also the author, has a kind of quasi-divine power and control.

The hope held out to Agnes, the other little girl in this "double story", is much bleaker. While Agnes's father is led off to salvation by the Wise Woman, her mother is told:

> "She [Agnes] is your crime and your punishment. Take her home with you, and live hour after hour with the pale-hearted disgrace you call your daughter. What she is, the worm at her heart has begun to teach her. When life is no longer endurable, come to me." (*CFT* 302)

This tiny beginning of wisdom in Agnes's heart has been brought about by another of the Wise Woman's tests which seem to make the latter, as Knoepflmacher has pointed out, "a distinct cousin of the cruel Watho" (*CFT* 187). For her own good, we are to understand, Agnes is placed naked into a "cunningly suspended" hollow sphere. She cannot escape, for wherever she walks, she remains in the same place, "like a squirrel in his cage" (*CFT* 259-60), MacDonald tells us. Space is thus effectively abolished for Agnes, but so also is time. Suspended in a sensory void, time disappears for Agnes:

> [N]othing to see but a cold blue light, and nothing to do but see it. Oh, how slowly the hours went by! She lost all notion of time. If she had been told that she had been there twenty years, she would have believed it—or twenty minutes—it would have been all the same: except for weariness, time was for her no more. (*CFT* 260)

In this timeless void, Agnes is confronted by herself in the form of an uncanny double, whom Agnes hates "with her whole heart". Discovering that she appears to be shut up with her own Self for ever and ever, Agnes falls asleep in "an agony of despair" (*CFT* 261). She awakes "sick at herself" and "would gladly have been put out of existence" (ibid.). On the third day, Agnes is beginning to see the truth about herself, and on the following morning she awakes in the arms of the Wise Woman, with "the horror" (that is, her Self) vanished (ibid.). However, despite the Wise Woman's warnings, Agnes soon lapses, and fails the tasks set her by the Wise Woman. She finally runs away and ends up as a scullery-maid in the palace kitchens. In a nice reversal of expectations, it is the princess who eventually learns humility, love and self-control, and not the peasant girl, whose only hope is "the worm at her heart"—in this Agnes prefigures the fate of Lilith.[23]

"The Wise Woman" may seem to be more directed towards parents than children. But to reverse—yet paradoxically maintain—MacDonald's characteristic attitude towards his readers: it is for grown-ups of all ages. The fashionable term "crossover" is eminently applicable to MacDonald, who might well insist, like the Wise Woman herself, that in all the different interpretations he receives (from those aged five to those of seventy-five): "It always is me, all the time". (*CFT* 294) As Princess Irene's great-great-grandmother (also of course called Princess Irene) tells Curdie in chapter 7 of *The Princess and Curdie*, entitled "What *is* in a Name?":

> "You may ask me as many questions as you please—that is, as long as they are sensible. Only I may take a few thousand years to answer some of them. But that's nothing. *Of all things time is the cheapest.*' (*PGPC* 208; emphasis added)

This is a shocking saying, scandalous to those of us who constantly fear the loss of what we perceive (or are conditioned to perceive) as the most precious and expensive of all commodities, time. The Lady, who appears sublimely indifferent to questions of "time-management", replies to Curdie's baffled questions about the relativistic implications of her constant shape-shifting: "Shapes are only dresses, Curdie, and dresses are only names. That which is inside is the same all the time". Which, uncannily enough, brings me full circle, back to the beginning of this essay and to the philosophical paper I gave at Roehampton seven years ago, a paper which, like most philosophical essays in the Western tradition, was ultimately concerned with the old Platonic problems of the One and the

---

[23] See George MacDonald, *Lilith* (Grand Rapids: Eerdmans, 1981), p.201. See also Chapter Two above, "The Angel in the House of Death: Gender and Subjectivity in George MacDonald's *Lilith*".

Many, of Identity and Difference, of Being and Time.[24] For, as A.N. Whitehead once provocatively said, European philosophy is a series of footnotes to Plato.[25] But so too, arguably, is European literature, including, and perhaps even especially, European children's literature.

---

[24] The paper was published as "Interpretation Theory and Performance: Gadamer/Derrida/Nietzsche" in the electronic journal *Signatures* Vol. 2 Winter 2000 [http://www.chiuni.ac.uk/info/Signatures.cfm]
[25] A.N. Whitehead, *Process and Reality: An Essay on Cosmology* (Gifford Lectures at the University of Edinburgh, 1927-8) (Cambridge: Cambridge University Press, 1929), p.53.

WORKS CITED

Abrams, M. H. *Natural supernaturalism: Tradition and Revolution in Romantic Literature.* New York: Norton, 1973.

Saint Augustine. *Confessions.* Trans. Henry Chadwick. Oxford: Oxford University Press, 1992.

Balfour, Graham. *The Life of Robert Louis Stevenson.* One Volume Edition. London: Methuen, 1906.

Beckett, Samuel. *Waiting for Godot.* London: Faber and Faber, 1965.

Bloom, Harold. *The Anxiety of Influence.* New York: Oxford University Press, 1973.

—. *A Map of Misreading.* New York: Oxford University Press, 1975.

—. *The Flight to Lucifer: a Gnostic Fantasy*, New York: Farrar, 1979.

—. *"Clinamen*: Towards a Theory of Fantasy." in E. Slusser, E. Rabkin and R. Scholes (eds.). *Bridges to Fantasy.* Carbondale: Southern Illinois University Press, 1982.

Booth, Bradford A., and Mehew, Ernest (eds). *The Letters of Robert Louis Stevenson.* 8 volumes. New Haven: Yale University Press, 1994-5.

Bowie, Andrew. *Aesthetics and Subjectivity: From Kant to Nietzsche.* 2nd ed. Manchester: Manchester University Press, 2003.

Brown, Peter. *Augustine of Hippo.* London: Faber, 1967.

Bultmann, Rudolf. *New Testament and Mythology and Other Basic Writings.* Ed and trans. by Schubert M. Ogden. Augsburg: Fortress, 1984.

Carlyle, Thomas. "Novalis" in *Critical and Miscellaneous Essays.* Vol. 2 London: Chapman and Hall, 1899.

Cusick, Edmund. "George MacDonald and Jung." in William Raeper (ed.). *The Gold Thread: Essays on George MacDonald.* Edinburgh: Edinburgh University Press, 1990.

Dante, Alighieri. *The Divine Comedy.* See under Musa.

Derrida, Jacques. *Of Grammatology.* Trans. Gayatri Spivak. Baltimore: John Hopkins University Press, 1975.

Dickinson, Emily. *The Complete Poems.* Ed. Thomas H. Johnson. London: Faber and Faber, 1975.

Dyregrov, A. *Grief in Children.* London: Jessica Kingsley, 2007.

Durie, Catherine. "George MacDonald and C.S. Lewis." in William Raeper (ed.). *The Gold Thread: Essays on George MacDonald.* Edinburgh: Edinburgh University Press, 1990.

Filoramo, Giovanni. *A History of Gnosticism.* Oxford: Blackwell, 1990.

Freud, Sigmund. "The Uncanny." *Art and Literature.* Penguin Freud Library vol. 14. London: Penguin, 1990.

Furnas, J.C. *Voyage to Windward.* London: Faber & Faber, 1952.

Gadamer, Hans-Georg. *Philosophical Hermeneutics.* Berkeley: University of California Press, 1977.

—. *Truth and Method.* Trans. Weinsheimer and Marshall. New ed. New York: Continuum, 2004.

Gibb, Jocelyn, ed. *Light on C.S. Lewis.* London: Geoffrey Bles, 1965.

Gilbert, Sandra M., and Gubar, Susan. *The Madwoman in the Attic: The Woman Writer and the Nineteenth-century Literary Imagination.* New Haven: Yale University Press, 1979.

Goethe, Johann Wolfgang von. *Faust, Part One.* Trans. David Luke. Oxford: Oxford University Press, 1981.

Gray, William. *C.S. Lewis.* Plymouth: Northcote House, 1998.

—. "Interpretation Theory and Performance: Gadamer/Derrida/Nietzsche." In the electronic journal *Signatures* Vol. 2 Winter 2000 [http://www.chiuni.ac.uk/info/Signatures.cfm]

—. *Robert Louis Stevenson: A Literary Life.* London and Basingstoke: Palgrave Macmillan, 2004.

—. *Fantasy, Myth and the Measure of Truth: Tales of Pullman, Lewis, Tolkien, MacDonald and Hoffmann.* London and Basingstoke: Palgrave Macmillan, 2008.

Haill, Lyn (ed.). *Darkness Illuminated.* London: National Theatre / Oberon Books, 2004.

Hardy, Elizabeth Baird. *Milton, Spenser and the Chronicles of Narnia: Literary Sources for the C.S. Lewis Novels.* Jefferson, N.C.: McFarland, 2007.

Hayward, Deidre. "The Mystical Sophia: More on the Great Grandmother in the Princess Books." *North Wind: Journal of George MacDonald Studies*, 13, 1994.

Heidegger, Martin. *Being and Time.* Trans. John Macquarrie and Edward Robinson. New York: Harper, 1962.

Holbrook, David. Introduction to George MacDonald. *Phantastes.* London: Everyman Paperback, 1983.

—. *The Skeleton in the Wardrobe: C.S. Lewis' Fantasies: A Phenomenological Study.* Lewisburg: Bucknell University Press, 1991.

—. *A Study of George Macdonald and the Image of Woman*. New York: Edwin Mellen, 2000.

Holland, Norman N. "Literary Interpretation and Three Phases of Psychoanalysis." *CritI* 3, 2 Winter 1976. Reprinted in Alan Roland (ed.). *Psychoanalysis, Creativity and Literature*. New York: Columbia University Press, 1978.

Hurwitz, Siegmund. *Lilith: The First Eve*. Einsiedeln: Daimon Verlag, 1992.

Jackson, Rosemary. *Fantasy: the Literature of Subversion*. London: Methuen, 1981.

Jacobs, Alan. *The Narnian: The Life and Imagination of C.S. Lewis*. New York: HarperCollins, 2005.

Jenkins, Ruth Y. "'I am spinning this for you, my child': Voice and Identity Formation in George MacDonald's Princess Books." *The Lion and the Unicorn*, September 2004 Vol. 28, No. 3.

Johnson, Barbara. "The Frame of Reference." *Yale French Studies* 55/56, 1977.

Jonas, Hans. *The Gnostic Religion: The Message of the Alien God and the Beginnings of Christianity*. 2nd rev. ed. Boston: Beacon Press, 1963.

Joseph, Gerhard and Tucker, Herbert F., "Passing On: Death" in Herbert F. Tucker (ed.). *A Companion to Victorian Literature And Culture*.Oxford: Blackwell, 1999.

Kegler, Adelheid. "Einhundert Lichtjahre in neunzehn Stunden: Das rätselhafte Raumschiff in David Lindsay's *A Voyage to Arcturus*." *Inklings-Jahrbuch* 21 2003.

King, Shelley. "'Without Lyra we would understand neither the New nor the Old Testament': Exegesis, Allegory and Reading *The Golden Compass*." in Millicent Lenz with Carole Scott (eds). *His Dark Materials Illuminated: Critical Essays on Philip Pullman's Trilogy*. Detroit: Wayne State University Press, 2005.

Knoepflmacher, U.C. (ed.). *George MacDonald: The Complete Fairy Tales*. Harmondsworth: Penguin, 1999.

Kristeva, Julia. *Revolution in Poetic Language*. Trans. Margaret Waller. New York: Columbia University Press, 1984.

—. "Women's Time." in Toril Moi (ed.). *The Kristeva Reader*. Oxford: Blackwell, 1986.

—. *Powers of Horror: An Essay on Abjection*. Trans. Leon S. Roudiez. New York: Columbia University Press, 1982.

—. *Tales of Love*. Trans. Leon S. Roudiez. New York: Columbia University Press, 1987.

—. *Black Sun: Depression and Melancholia*. Trans. Leon S. Roudiez. New York: Columbia University Press, 1989.

Koltuv, Barbara. *The Book of Lilith*. York Beach, Maine: Nicholas-Hays, 1986.

Lacan, Jacques. *The Four Fundamental Concepts of Psychoanalysis: The Seminar of Jacques Lacan: Book XI*. Ed. Jacques-Alain Miller; trans. Alan Sheridan. New York: Norton, 1998.

Layton, Bentley (ed). *The Gnostic Scriptures: A New Translation with Annotations and Introductions*. London : SCM, 1987.

Lechte, John *Julia Kristeva*. London: Routledge, 1990.

Leitch, Vincent, et al., (eds). *The Norton Anthology of Theory and Criticism*. New York: Norton, 2001.

Lenz, Millicent, with Scott, Carole (eds.). *His Dark Materials Illuminated: Critical Essays on Philip Pullman's Trilogy*. Detroit: Wayne State University Press, 2005.

Lewis, C.S. *The Pilgrim's Regress: An Allegorical Apology for Christianity, Reason and Romanticism*. Revised edition. London: Geoffrey Bles, 1943.

—. *George MacDonald: An Anthology*. London: Geoffrey Bles, 1946.

—. *The Cosmic Trilogy: Out of the Silent Planet*; *Perelandra*; *That Hideous Strength*. London: Pan Books in association with The Bodley Head, 1989.

—. *The Screwtape Letters*. London: Collins Fontana, 1955.

—. *The Lion, the Witch and the Wardrobe*. London: HarperCollins, 1996.

—. *The Magician's Nephew*. Harmondsworth: Puffin, 1963.

—. *The Last Battle*. London: HarperCollins, 1997.

—. *Surprised by Joy: The shape of my early life*. London: Fontana, 1959.

—. *An Experiment in Criticism*. Cambridge: Cambridge University Press, 1961.

—. *Letters to Malcolm: Chiefly on Prayer*. London: Collins Fount, 1977.

—. *A Grief Observed*. London: Faber, 1966.

—. *Selected Literary Essays*. Ed. Walter Hooper. Cambridge: Cambridge University Press, 1969.

—. *Selected Books*. London: HarperCollins, 2002.

—. *Of This and Other Worlds*. London: Collins, 1982.

—. *They Stand Together: The Letters of C. S. Lewis to Arthur Greeves 1914-1963*. Ed. Walter Hooper. London: Collins, 1979.

Lewis C.S., and Tillyard, E.M.W. *The Personal Heresy: A Controversy*. London: Oxford University Press, 1939.

Lindsay, David. *A Voyage to Arcturus* Edinburgh: Canongate Classics, 1998.

Logan, A.H.B. *The Gnostics: Identifying an Ancient Christian Cult.* Edinburgh: T. and T. Clark, 2006.

MacDonald, George. *Phantastes: A Faërie Romance.* London: Dent (Everyman), 1915.

—. *Lilith.* Grand Rapids: Eerdmans, 1981.

—. *The Princess and the Goblin* and *The Princess and Curdie.* Ed. R. McGillis. Oxford: Oxford University Press, 1990.

—. *The Poetical Works of George MacDonald.* Vol. II. London: Chatto & Windus, 1893.

—. *The Complete Fairy Tales.* See under Knoepflmacher.

MacDonald, Greville. *George MacDonald and His Wife.* London: George Allen and Unwin, 1924.

Manlove, C. N. *Modern Fantasy: Five Studies.* Cambridge: Cambridge University Press, 1975.

McGillis, Roderick. "*Phantastes and Lilith:* Femininity and Freedom" in William Raeper (ed.). *The Gold Thread.* Edinburgh: Edinburgh University Press, 1990.

Menikoff, Barry, *Robert Louis Stevenson and 'The Beach of Falesá': A Study in Victorian Publishing.* Stanford: Stanford University Press, 1984.

Moi, Toril (ed.). *The Kristeva Reader.* Oxford: Blackwell, 1986.

Monaco, James. *How to read a film: language, history, theory.* 3rd ed. Oxford: Oxford University Press, 2000.

Murdoch, Iris. *The Fire and the Sun: Why Plato Banished the Artists.* Oxford: Oxford University Press, 1977.

Musa, Mark (trans, and ed.). *The Portable Dante.* New York: Penguin, 1995.

Myers, Doris T. *C.S.Lewis in Context.* Kent State University Press, 1994.

Novalis. *Schriften.* Ed. Kluckhohn and Samuel. Dritter Band. Stuttgart: Kohlhammer, 1960.

Nuttall, A.D. *A New Mimesis.* London: Methuen, 1983.

Oliver, Kelly. *Reading Kristeva: Unraveling the Double-bind.* Bloomington: Indiana University Press, 1993.

Otto, Rudolf. *The Idea of the Holy.* Trans. John W. Harvey. 2nd ed. Oxford: Oxford University Press, 1950.

Pagels, Elaine. *The Gnostic Gospels.* Harmondsworth: Penguin, 1981.

—. *Adam, Eve and the Serpent.* Harmondsworth: Penguin, 1990.

Parsons, Wendy, and Nicholson, Catriona. "Talking to Philip Pullman: An Interview." *The Lion and the Unicorn* 23: 1 January 1999.

Pearce, Lynne. *Woman/Image/Text: Readings in Pre-Raphaelite Art and Literature.* London: Harvester Wheatsheaf, 1991.

Prickett, Stephen. "Fictions and Metafictions: 'Phantastes,' 'Wilhelm Meister,' and the idea of the 'Bildungsroman,'" in William Raeper (ed.). *The Gold Thread*. Edinburgh: Edinburgh University Press, 1990.

Pullman, Philip. *Northern Lights* (= *The Golden Compass*). London: Scholastic, 1995.

—. *Clockwork*. London: Corgi Yearling, 1997.

—. *Count Karlstein or The Ride of the Deman Huntsman*. London: Corgi Yearling, 1998.

—. *I Was a Rat!: or The Scarlet Slippers*. London: Corgi Yearling, 2000.

—. *The Amber Spyglass*. London: Scholastic, 2000.

—. "A word or two about myths." *The Myths Boxset*. Edinburgh: Canongate, 2005.

William Raeper. *George MacDonald*. Tring: Lion, 1987..

William Raeper (ed.). *The Gold Thread: Essays on George MacDonald*. Edinburgh: Edinburgh University Press, 1990.

Rayment-Pickard, Hugh. *The Devil's Account: Philip Pullman and Christianity*. London: Darton Longman and Todd, 2004.

Raymond, Marcel. *From Baudelaire to Surrealism*. London: Methuen, 1970.

Reis, Richard. *George MacDonald*. New York: Twayne Books, 1972.

Robb, David S. *George MacDonald*. Edinburgh: Scottish Academic Press, 1987.

Robinson, James M. (ed.). *The Nag Hammadi Library in English*. Leiden: Brill, 1977.

Rudolph, Kurt. *Gnosis: The Nature and History of Gnosticism*. Edinburgh: T. and T. Clark, 1983.

Speece, M.W., and Brent, S.B. "Children's Understanding of Death." *Journal of Child Development* Vol.55 1984.

Squires, Claire. *Philip Pullman's His Dark Materials' Trilogy*. London: Continuum, 2004.

Stevenson, Robert Louis. *The Strange Case of Dr Jekyll and Mr Hyde; Fables*. Tusitala Edition vol.5. London: Heinemann, 1924.

—. *Island Nights' Entertainments*. Tusitala Edition vol.13. London: Heinemann, 1924.

—. *The Siverado Squatters*. Tusitala Edition vol.18. London: Heinemann, 1924.

—. *In the South Seas*. Tusitala Edition vol.20. London: Heinemann, 1924.

—. "A Chapter on Dreams" in *Further Memories*. Tusitala Edition vol. 30. London: Heinemann, 1924.

—. *The Letters of Robert Louis Stevenson*. Vol. 1 Edited by Sidney Colvin. Tusitala Edition vol.31. London: Heinemann, 1924.

Stoljar, Margaret Mahoney (trans. and ed.). *Novalis: Philosophical Writings*. Albany: SUNY Press, 1997.

Thacker, Deborah Cogan, and Webb, Jean. *Introducing Children's Literature: from Romanticism to Postmodernism*. London: Routledge, 2002.

Tolkien, J.R.R. *Tree and Leaf; Smith of Wootton Major; The Homecoming of Beorhtnoth*. London: Unwin, 1975.

—. *The Monster and the Critics and Other Essays*. Edited by Christopher Tolkien. London: HarperCollins, 2006.

Walker, Andrew, and Patrick, James (eds). *A Christian for All Christians: Essays in Honour of C. S. Lewis*. London: Hodder and Stoughton, 1990.

Whitehead, A.N. *Process and Reality: An Essay on Cosmology*. Gifford Lectures at the University of Edinburgh, 1927-8. Cambridge: Cambridge University Press, 1929.

Wilson, A.N. *C. S. Lewis: A Biography*. London: Collins, 1990.

Winnicott, D. W. *The Maturational Process and the Facilitating Environment*. London: Hogarth, 1965.

—. *Home is Where We Start From*. Harmondsworth: Penguin, 1986.

Wolff, Robert Lee. *The Golden Key: A Study of the Fiction of George MacDonald*. New Haven: Yale University Press 1961.

Woolf, Virginia. "Professions for Women." in Stephen Greenblatt and M.H. Abrams (eds). *The Norton Anthology of English Literature* Vol. 2 (Eighth Edition). New York: W.W. Norton, 2006.

Zipes, Jack (ed.). *The Oxford Companion to Fairy Tales*. Oxford: Oxford University Press, 2000.

INDEX

Stevenson, Robert Louis, 3, 4, 35-
    51
  Fables, 50, 51
  Island Nights' Entertainments,
    43-50
  *Strange Case of Dr Jekyll and
    Mr Hyde*, 3, 39, 40, 50, 64
Swedenborg, Emanuel, 100
Thacker, Deborah, 88n, 99n
Todorov, Tzvetan, 4, 48
J.R.R. Tolkien, 36, 54, 89, 97
  The Lord of the Rings, 94
  "On Fairy-Stories", 1, 4, 54n,
    59, 73n, 75, 81, 82, 87
Tucker, Herbert H., 2n
Webb, Jean, 88n, 99n
Weber, Carl Maria von, 99
Weil, Simone, 69
White, Gleeson, 41, 42n
Whitehead, A.N., 114
Whitman, Walt, 37

Wilde, Oscar, 38
Wlliams, Rowan, 88n, 100
Wilson, A.N., 71n
Wimsatt, W.K and Beardsley,
    Monroe C., 66
  "The Intentional Fallacy", 66
Winnicott, D.W., 5, 10, 11, 18, 33,
    76, 77, 80, 83
  Home is Where We Start From,
    33n
  *The Maturational Process
    and the Facilitating
    Environment*, 33n, 83n
Wittgenstein, Ludwig, 55
Wolff, Robert Lee, 9, 10, 27
Woolf, Virginia, 3, 25, 26, 29, 102
Wordsworth, William, 54, 92, 100,
    107
Yeats, W.B., 81n, 109
Zipes, Jack, 44n, 46n, 48n